Marly Youmans

THE CURSE OF THE RAVEN MOCKER

It's been weeks since Adanta's sick father left on a quest to find the healing lake mentioned in the lore of the Cherokee. Since then a visitor has arrived, a man Adanta doesn't like – James, or, as she's styled him, the Lean One. One day, after witnessing him make a frightening incantation, Adanta finds that her mother has fallen under the Lean One's spell, and she is lured away from the cottage. Left alone in a remote area of the Smoky Mountains, Adanta has no choice but to venture forth into the wilderness, in the hope of finding both her parents. To accomplish this, she must journey to Adantis, the secret home of the Hidden People deep in the mountains.

On her quest, Adanta finds many friends, but she also encounters untold dangers, including the threat of the Raven Mockers – humans who take the form of birds and steal the remaining life from those who are hurt or ill. To protect herself, and potentially save her mother and be reunited with her father, will require all the strength and courage she can muster.

MARLY YOUMANS is the author of three previous novels for adults. She lives in Cooperstown, New York.

THE *CURSE* OF THE *RAVEN MOCKER*

THE CURSE OF THE
RAVEN MOCKER

MARLY YOUMANS

FARRAR STRAUS GIROUX　　NEW YORK

Copyright © 2003 by Marly Youmans
All rights reserved
Distributed in Canada by Douglas & McIntyre Ltd.
Printed in the United States of America
Designed by Jennifer Crilly
First edition, 2003
1 3 5 7 9 10 8 6 4 2

Library of Congress Cataloging-in-Publication Data
Youmans, Marly.
The curse of the Raven Mocker / Marly Youmans.— 1st ed.
p. cm.
Summary: After her parents disappear from their isolated home in the Great
Smoky Mountains, Adanta discovers the truth of the Cherokee stories her father
told her and embarks on a journey to thwart the sorcery that has claimed her
parents.
ISBN 0-374-31667-8
[1. Cherokee mythology—Fiction. 2. Supernatural—Fiction. 3. Wizards—
Fiction. 4. Indians of North America—Southern States—Folklore—Fiction.
5. Great Smoky Mountains (N.C. and Tenn.)—Fiction.] I. Title.

PZ7.Y843 Cu 2003
[Fic]—dc21

2002026433

Come away, O human child!
To the waters and the wild
With a faery, hand in hand,
For the world's more full of weeping
than you can understand.

—W. B. YEATS, "THE STOLEN CHILD"

CONTENTS

THE CURSE OF THE RAVEN MOCKER

THE BLUE ROAD

Under the great folds of the mountains that are known as the Blue Ridge because they are often the color of twilight—and that are in places called the Smokies because they send up a blue fume into the sky—there is a spot that is still almost unsettled, a cove with only a few lawns notched in its slopes. There, in the doorway of the house that her mother had named the Little Cottage In Between, the girl Adanta was standing, shoeless, one foot on the sill and one on the grass beyond. It was already summer, and the bees buzzed in the small crammed garden on each side of the door, but Adanta was not thinking about their songs or the bright hollyhocks and roses. She shivered lightly, stepping out into the sunshine. The whole air of the place seemed changed to her: it felt tighter, as if strung with a thousand taut wires, and slightly electric, as if humming with invisible messages. When a big black bird flashed from its hiding place in a sourwood tree, she flinched, putting up one hand.

Just a bird.

The Lean One had come seven days ago, and for the last three now she had been watching and following his movements. She had to find out what it was he wanted, what ill thing he meant to do. That he intended to do harm she felt certain. But he had not touched her, nor her mother, and it seemed that Charlotte welcomed him. Where did he go, when he was not with them? He would slip away, and she could not find him anywhere, not in the outbuildings or the woods or at the pool where she had seen him bathe. He neither ate nor drank nor slept in the house. Often he seemed to escape her vigilance as if by magic. Right now she did not know where he was but sensed that he was near.

At times, Adanta was unsure whether she watched him—or whether it might be the other way around. The idea made her feel twitchy, and she wanted to gallop yelling down the slope into the valley, like an animal driven to panic by a biting fly.

There! Something: it faded away in white fluttery

glimpses, like a wreath of flowers bobbing on a stream half-hidden by trees. The girl trembled, and in her very bones she felt watery, suddenly unable to run.

"Move like the current when you want to come and go unheard." Those were her father's words; now that he was gone, such recollections were what remained of him.

She squeezed her eyes shut.

An instant later, she opened them again, the glaring landscape of midday flashing dark and light. The whiteness among the trunks of trees had almost vanished, wobbling into the distance.

After another moment in which she tensed and drew herself up, Adanta sped off, heedless of the catbriers that slashed at her legs, the slap of leaves across her face, or the tinder of needles splayed underfoot. Once she stopped, panting, to listen: nothing but the sough of branches. She was gaining on the mothlike patch of white, and she guessed that the Lean One was returning to the pool where she had seen him splash and dive on the two days before. Stopping, she leaned against a pine, pressing her palms against the fragmented bark and the resin, and waited until her breath slowed.

"Like the current," she whispered, looking up at the star of sun and an island of blue showing between tall boles.

Now she weaved more quietly through the trees, arcing the long way around toward the pond fed by jagged rivulets of ice water, springing straight from the rock. He could not hear her by that path, not unless he had the hearing of a wild beast.

When she crawled to the far lip of the shore, sheltering behind a tangle of mountain laurel, she could see that he had bathed quickly this time and had already bound one of her mother's towels around his waist and pulled on the faded flannel shirt that made her think of Ba. On his hair was a ring of flowers, not tilted back but set over his brow like a crown. Kneeling, he marked his face below the eyes with a piece of burnt charcoal fished from a scattered campfire on the rocks. As he began to mumble, she pushed closer, crawling into a mess of jewelweed by the water's edge. She strained to hear every word over the spatter and drip of the waterfall, the flow sparse after a month of little rain.

His hands swept the air; his words became louder and more distinct.

"*Ku!* Listen! Snow Woman in Elahiyi, hear me! Make me a man of snowy whiteness so that no one is ever lonely with me. Paint a path like snow for me; put me in that path. Never let it grow blue with twilight."

The words hackled the fine hairs on Adanta's arms, along her spine. The tone didn't sound familiar, was harsher and hoarser than the one she knew as his; nor had she heard him speak in such a formal way.

His voice rose once more as he whirled about, hands upraised.

"Give me the snow-white road from above; set me there. Let me be handsome and strong always; let me live forever. Cover me with the snow of your house like a cloak."

At this, he pulled the coronet of flowers from his head and flung it onto the pool, where it bobbled on the surface. He stopped to watch, then began to stalk back and forth on the border of stones, his voice ringing.

"Now make the woman blue; make her path a road into twilight. Let her be veiled in loneliness. Set her feet on blue. Bring her down. Wherever she goes, let loneliness strike. Set her apart in blue."

Adanta crouched lower, flattening herself against moss and rocks and silt, pressing her face into the stems and leaves of jewelweed. *The blue woman.*

Breathing shallowly, she stared, her eyes fixed on the pacing figure, her heart jumping against the damp, chilled stones of the margin like a trapped newt, frantic to be free.

"Ha! Let my clan, the Wolf clan, be hers. Let me shine like sun on snow. Other men—let them be wraiths on the blue road. But let me stand with my face to the Sun Land. Never let me be the color of blue."

He faced east, toward the hidden cottage, stretching out his arms like wings and shouting, "Let her soul come into the core of my soul, never to turn away!"

As if hurled up by a sudden, icy wave, Adanta flew to her feet, shrieking at the man she had nicknamed the Lean One. Instantly she squatted down again, scrabbling in the dirt, forcing up smooth cobbles and bits of quartz to hurl. She lobbed them wildly, and they splashed into the water, a few striking the opposite shore and bounding away into the woods.

The Lean One swung his head around, smiling, as if he had been waiting for and expecting her full attention. Keeping his eyes upon her face, he backed up a few steps and reached his hands out in the direction of the cottage. Only then did he loosen his gaze from hers and turn away.

"Woman, your soul has come into my soul by the sacred rites of old. Neither child nor man nor the dead can hold you. I, Astugataga, take your soul. It is done!"

With a great cry, halfway between an animal's roar and a laugh of triumph, the Lean One swept up his remaining clothes and dashed off through the woods, his jeans trailing behind him like a banner.

The blue road.

The words lent a chilliness to the air, which had felt warm and close until then. Adanta realized that she was drenched in sweat. As if feverish, she bent over, chafing her arms, and all her limbs seemed enchanted to liquid once more. That wasn't what Ba had meant when he had told her to move like the current. The veins trickling in the mountain rocks held the power to flow quietly or to heave and crack stone, but she had been seen, maybe even lured to the spot as a witness, and she had ended by feeling as weak as tap water, trembling in a glass.

Set her feet on the blue road. The circlet of pale flowers that had rocked on the unsettled surface of the pool now was logged by spray and sank, at first showing dimly through the green. Then it was swallowed by the dark as it settled downward. What did it all mean? She was afraid, uncertain whether the

Lean One's words were a charm or a curse. And who was the woman? Did he mean her mother, whom his eyes were always assessing? Whom Adanta loved more than anything alive in the world except Ba, because although she had once loved them the same, lately she thought that she loved Ba more because she was losing him. *Neither child nor man nor the dead can hold you.* If it was Mama that the Lean One wanted, then Adanta must be the child and Ba the— the man? the dead? Tears trembled in Adanta's eyes.

Glancing down, she saw that there was blood under her fingernails, the tender skin beneath cut by the sand and the minute shards of rubies that salted the mountain streams.

Only for an instant did she rinse her hands; she started back to the house, walking, trotting, tearing along faster than anyone should in a forest where there are rattlesnakes and sinkholes and gnarly roots of trees to harm a runner.

She found Charlotte sitting in the window seat near the chimney, forehead resting against a glass pane. Adanta looked at her face and saw that she had been crying. Pausing, the glimmering of an idea in her mind, the girl looked at the window—like all the others in the cottage, it was outlined in a deep, vibrant blue. It had been her mother's thought to follow an old country practice and paint the frames blue to keep witches and sorcerers from crossing the threshold.

"Why didn't you make the doorway blue?" she asked slowly.

Charlotte looked up, her eyes drifting across Adanta's face.

"What do you mean?"

"Well, couldn't they get in the door—wizards and such?"

"I suppose, if there were such creatures. It's just an interesting custom." Her voice sounded dull, tired.

Blue, thought Adanta, her heart a rapid drumbeat in her chest.

"What happened to the rest of that paint?" she persisted. She could do it. There were brushes in a bucket out back, and a short ladder leaned against the side of the house, still waiting for Ba to feel better, to finish adding a second coat of buttery yellow onto the Little Cottage In Between.

"The garden shed. A cupboard with tarps and turpentine. Maybe there."

And so Adanta found the can with the lid jammed tight and pried it up, spilling paint on her shaking hands. She daubed the blue all around the white doorframe and across the sill, then went back over the whole thing, covering every inch of wood. Afterward she dragged the ladder away and stowed the can in the shed before scrubbing her hands.

Back in the house, her mother looked half-asleep, still hunched in the window seat, her eyes on the mountains. A whittling knife and a piece of basswood lay beside her, untouched.

"Mother," Adanta said.

She seemed too weary to answer.

"Please," the girl insisted.

"What is it?"

"I don't like him. Make him go away."

"Who?"

"Mother, you know who—*him*—the Lean One."

"Don't call him that," she protested mildly.

"Okay, then: Astugataga."

"James."

"Fine, Mama. Just make him go."

"He's your godfather."

"That can't be true."

"I had forgotten it myself, until he said . . . You can have two godfathers, you know, and James reminded me that he had been invited but couldn't come." Charlotte put a hand to her temple. "I had forgotten.

But I must have known. I remember that time when he came to visit for an hour. A strange visit."

"In what way?"

Charlotte went on without answering the question, still cauled in her own thoughts. "That was just before your father moved us to the Little Cottage, although we were happy and had so many friends where we were. It was all so quick. So abrupt."

"Maybe he didn't want the Lean One—James—to know where we lived? Did you ever think of that?"

"He *was* your father's playmate. Jess told me." Charlotte began fiddling with the knife, spinning it on the seat cushion. When the blade nicked her finger, she hardly noticed.

"Mama, people change. I don't think Ba would like him now."

But Charlotte was not listening. She stared at the fresh cut as if she did not know what it was, then looked away to the ridgeline.

"Make him go." Adanta placed a hand on her mother's shoulder.

"I can't. He's your father's—" Charlotte broke off. The Lean One was coming, dressed in jeans and the blue flannel shirt, the white towel around his neck.

Adanta stared at her mother. She did not look anything more than very attentive, but even that much response was alarming, after what had been seen and heard at the creek.

"Well," he drawled, one hand on hip, "looks like Miss Adanta is mad at me. Just plumb mad." He grinned mockingly at her. "Why don't you come outside, Charlotte, so she doesn't have to see my rotten, no-good face."

"No," Adanta whispered, "don't go."

"Come on. I don't want to spoil her precious blue paint."

"My daughter—" began Charlotte.

"She'll be all right. She's just mad at me, like I said. Come on out."

"No," Adanta repeated, leaning over to whisper. "He's not right. Something's wrong. He was saying things in the forest—he won't go through the blue door. Maybe he can't. Maybe he's a wizard, an evil wizard."

"How silly," Charlotte said dreamily, her eyes resting on the Lean One, who was, indeed, handsome enough to draw glances. Like her father, he was tall and slim, but his hair and skin were darker. He might be half Cherokee and half a descendant of the old settlers of the valleys.

"Mama," she said.

The Lean One came close, tugging on the wooden frame to the window screen; it popped free. Adanta hardly saw how her mother slipped down to the grass of the side yard, leaving behind only a drop of blood.

"Mama—" she called.

Her mother turned slightly, so that the girl could see the plane of her cheek.

"It's fine," she said in a low voice.

While Adanta watched, the two drifted off toward the trees and ducked under a low-hanging branch.

"Mama!" she shouted, climbing up on the seat and jumping down to the yard.

It was a mystery to her still. They had not been walking more than a few moments, yet no one was there on the path up the hill. Adanta had called and called and wept, standing in the middle of the clearing, but no one had ever answered. Her mother was gone, just as surely as if a whirlwind had lifted her up and planted her in some entirely different kingdom of the world.

THE LITTLE COTTAGE IN BETWEEN

So she had been alone for three days, and so she seemed likely to continue. The bees went on making their wildflower-and-sourwood honey in the bee boxes on the slope. The garden went on blooming. Yet everything was changed. *I'm just a child, really,* Adanta thought, *and all this has happened to me.* She paused, listening to the rustling of the cornstalks. *What is it they want to say?*

I will wait until the food is almost gone, she decided. *Then I will go down to the Messers' farm no matter what, because I don't think*—she no longer felt entirely sure—*that my mother would want me to be hungry. And after that I will find Ba and Mama, and I will bring them back whether it takes me seven days or seven years.*

There. She felt better, having made a choice. From

the Messers' corn maze came a gunshot, another: a flock of black birds soared upward. Adanta watched them swoop, their far-off jeers barely audible. They skidded downward, *cr-u-kking*, and she gave a little shake, remembering how the Raven Mockers were said to cry out against the dying, their fiery wings shedding sparks in the night. Had one soared down to her father's side and plucked out his life, somewhere in the mountains? Adanta rubbed her arms, cold even in the sunny doorway. The world was a strange place. Still, here were the bees furred with golden pollen and the yard shouting with bright flowers, and off in the next cove were the little white church where her mother's family members lay buried and the school where her father had been a teacher. Maybe she would go there and ask for help. She shivered, wondering if she would end up as somebody's foster child. No, she couldn't; she needed to search for Ba, for Mama. Another blast broke into her thoughts, and this time the black birds rose up as a body and swooped across the cove. Shading her eyes, Adanta watched them scatter into the dark trees.

Her glance strayed farther down the valley, past the slanting upper fields to where the Messers' plots made green splotches in the forest, and came to rest on the big corn maze. From her vantage point the field appeared a corrugated pattern that only gradually could be made out as the reclining Corn Woman, a bear, and a cucumber vine.

I could go down to the Messer place, she thought, but shook her head. Her mother had never liked them much.

It almost seemed that she could hear the huge hybrid cornstalks whispering across the valley. Adanta turned slowly in a circle. Nothing as far as she could see. Still, she could hear a faint rustling in the air, and she looked once more over her shoulder.

She was so unready to be alone!

I am still too young, she told herself. *My mother shouldn't have left me, not even for a day.*

Never had she known the hours to pass so slowly. Her eyes prickled and she let the lids close, then opened them again in alarm. What had she been thinking?

If only her father had never become ill with the blood sickness that sapped him and made him lie in the hammock or on the cool wooden floor for days at a time. It was the thing that had drawn him, first away from his friends after he had become too weak to teach at the school, and then away from his wife and child. If only the disease had not begun to pull him, so that, when he was up, he sat or stood near the edge of the clearing, staring toward the mountains—not toward the hamlets and towns strewn in their folds but toward the wilderness that the government and in some places the Cherokee held. Her father always said that no one owned the mountains, that it was a "rampant impossibility" to own a mountain—though the people in the villages thought that they owned the ridges, and they carved them and broke them and put up houses and fences and roads to mark the fact that they meant to own the very earth itself.

"A rampant impossibility," Adanta murmured and, after a moment, even smiled a little.

It was, she remembered, something in the deeps of the mountains that had called to her father. He had said that it called to his blood, wanted him to come away and throw himself down in a remote place where he would rise again, well and happy. It was the one-eighth part of himself, the Cherokee part, that wanted to go. Thanks to him, she was one-sixteenth Cherokee, although it showed nowhere except in her cheeks, or so her father said. "All the same, they will claim you, down to one-thirty-second and on beyond. They will claim you forever, to the end of time," he told her, after she had asked if it counted.

In the weeks before his journey, the sick man had become obsessed with an old Cherokee legend. "The healing lake," he had said to her mother, "Atagahi. The 'Gall Place.'"

He repeated the words several times, until Adanta could see that there were tears in her mother's eyes, and she wondered why he did not stop.

"There is no such spot," her mother told him. "None. It's only a myth. A story. Nothing more than that."

When he did not answer, she burst out, "Maybe it's your mother calling you—have you thought of that? You should go to church and pray for protection. Maybe something evil is luring you."

This was a mystery to Adanta—wasn't her grandmother dead? Hadn't she died when Adanta was a toddler, years back? Did her mother mean that a ghostly woman was summoning her father? If so, it seemed as much a "story" as Ba's belief in healing waters.

He paid no attention, walking across the lawn, leaning on his big sparkleberry staff.

For a long time he had stood looking out, and when he came back to the house at last, he appeared strange to Adanta—exalted somehow, and pale.

The next day he left home at dawn, when the

clouds still sit on the shoulders of the mountains and the coves are blue. Her mother's cries awakened Adanta, who lay in her canopy bed looking up at the white gauze, afraid to find out what had happened. Then a fear came over her that Jess was dead, and she would never again tramp the hills with him, learning the paw prints of animals and the names of the trees and plants. She bolted out of bed and sped through the empty house, slamming doors as she ran. Such a strange dream it seemed now, this fleeing into the cool dawn, the hem of an outgrown night-gown fluttering at her knees. She remembered racing past her mother, a bowed figure, the face marked with strain that might have been anger or grief, a few tears glittering on her cheeks. Stumbling over tree roots, she called to him, "It's me, Adanta, Adanta," because she could never bear for him to go anywhere without saying goodbye.

"Ba, come here, Ba," she shouted, growing desperate, calling him by the name she had used since infancy, the name he had never failed to answer.

And had she run smack into him? All she could remember was butting her head against the worn blue flannel of his shirt, leaning against him and holding on, smelling the familiar smell of him that now had been tainted by sickness for almost a year. He promised to be back in three weeks. Just twenty-one days. The shirt was dark over his heart, where she had pressed her wet cheek.

It had been a long time now, more than seven weeks.

Then her mother had vanished.

Repeatedly Adanta went over the time before her mother's disappearance, trying to explain to herself how such a thing could have happened, how it had all begun: at first, Charlotte had gone back to carving with a nervous fury. It was what she did, and it was what put bread on the table. All her life she had whittled. One year she had packed herself off to the Penland School to carve with a group of other "whittling fellows." Afterward her polished, traditional animal sculptures slowly became popular and eventually expensive enough so that they had few troubles with money, even after Ba had quit working.

It seemed to Adanta that Mama's unhappiness had begun before they moved to the Little Cottage In Between. Charlotte hadn't wanted to leave the old house, had liked having near neighbors and the noise of Adanta's playmates laughing and shouting through the high-ceilinged rooms. She had been the one to wake the girls early on May Day so that they could wash their faces in dew and be beautiful forever. At night she had often led a parade of boys and girls into the big meadow to chase fireflies and to stargaze. She had never lost her pleasure in sparklers, pot-and-spoon bands, crowns, silly hats, and shimmery capes, all of which featured in her evening adventures, and she had the gift of making these things seem magical yet comic, so that even the oldest children would join in. One summer she had wrapped the dead oak by the porch with a three-level tree house that Adanta and her friends called Maiden Castle, even though boys were allowed. Every week or so Charlotte would carve a new bird or insect into the dead branches to surprise the children, and troops of fairies whirled in frozen splendor about the trunk. But after the move she was lonely, disturbed that Jess wanted to cut off contact with the families they had known before.

She tried to settle in and please him, especially when he became ill. She and Adanta started a new tree house, stripped wallpaper from the bedrooms, and planted up the gardens. In good weather they dragged easels out onto the hills and painted the views, then tacked their pictures to the walls. When May Day came, they got up early and picked a basket of flowers but did not wash their faces in the dew. Only once had they gone out to catch fireflies and look at the stars, which seemed brighter here because the cove was so dark. It felt sad without the meadow and the children, and they didn't try again. Still, Charlotte was getting more work done than ever, and the vegetable plot lay deep in a mulch of shavings.

Looking back, Adanta thought that the constant whittling was a measure of her mother's efforts to carve a way out of discontent. And it only increased as Jess began talking of the enchanted lake. In the days after he had departed, she left a trail of shavings everywhere she went, as if she would whittle her troubles into peelings light enough for the wind to blow away.

Then everything changed; she slowed, stopped.

The Lean One came for her. *The Lean One*: that was what Adanta styled him, although his name was James, something simple and plain. Also, he called himself Astugataga, which he said was the name of a great warrior of the nineteenth century. He materialized at the edge of the clearing as if he had just been invented, for he looked new, startling, out-of-place in their lives. He was attractive, with high cheekbones and shining hair loose on his shoulders. There was nothing about him that appeared familiar to Adanta except his faded blue flannel, which gave her the creepy feeling that he might be wearing her ba's shirt. But surely there were plenty of comfortable old flannels in the world, many of them blue.

"Your godfather, your father's friend," Adanta's mother said, laughing, seizing his arm. Embracing the Lean One.

Adanta frowned, not putting out her hand.

"He hasn't seen you except once, just before—"

"It's been a while." The Lean One nodded, his eyes not on his godchild but on her mother. "Too long."

Charlotte hugged Adanta, squeezing her and whispering, "Did I ever tell you how much I love you?" It was more pleasure than she had shown in weeks.

He urged her mother to come with him—they would search for the missing man together, staying with people he knew back in the government lands.

"There are no people living there," she answered him, surprised. "Except a few—my husband's mother—a boy on a pony who showed up here—I suppose his family and one or two others."

He nodded. "That's what they want you to think. Charlotte, didn't Jess tell you about the Hidden People? The Hiddenites? His people, all mixed-up Irish and Scots and Cherokee?"

Adanta's mother stared at the Lean One.

"You must be mistaken—"

"They've been together since the Civil War," he added. "Some go even further back. They've got their own ways."

"I knew his mother was not—" Charlotte stopped, her gaze drifting to her daughter.

"Isn't my grandmother dead?" Adanta demanded.

"Don't speak of her!"

That moment Adanta could remember clearly, Mama backing away into a clump of snakeroot, and the Lean One beginning to smile with only one side of his mouth as he reached out a hand. It was then that it came to her that maybe this fellow James liked his friend's wife more than he should. She saw what she had never been forced to observe: that her mother was still young and lively, with thick hair and green eyes as changeable as water, with rosy cheeks and lips that needed no paint.

From then on, Adanta watched him closely, even following him at a distance when he went down to the creek pool to bathe and swim. She trailed him there, spying as he stripped to a loincloth and dived into the ice-cold water, rising with a gasp, flinging back his hair so that a fan of spray flew from his head. Sometimes it seemed that he knew she followed him, that he did not care or else might even be playing a game with her; sometimes the girl did not know what to think, but always she was alert and afraid.

And that was how a tale of vanishings had begun and had flourished, like a mighty plant sprung from a seed dropped by a raven in the gloom of the forest. Imagine its progress: tiny and seemingly harmless, it sleeps in the frosty earth until the next spring, when it sends up stems, the young leaves at first sulking in the shadows but later growing large and vigorous, feeding on soil and sun. Only later on do its purple blossoms or poisonous fruits make the passing traveler see that it was, all along, a sprout of deadly nightshade.

Again and again Adanta retraced the story, the weeks of Ba's absence and the seven days of the Lean One's visit, but the retelling always ended the same way, with the terrible close already set and known: the Lean One cursed Charlotte and took her away.

THE PONY BOY

Adanta fingered the hoop of wood around the mirror, carved with the figure of the sleeping Corn Woman, a rabbit and the moon, a wolf and a bear. When she met her own face, she saw a change in herself. There were her eyes, a curious reddish brown that matched the auburn hair, with darkness underneath that recent nights of wakefulness had left behind. Her skin was pale like her mother's, with a skift of freckles over the nose. All of her was slim; she still had the build of a girl who has grown quickly and who is swift and light as a bird.

The floor was cool to her bare feet as she turned, wandering restlessly through the cottage. It had begun to alter. A faint, almost invisible snow of dust covered everything, clouding the windows, softening the colors. Adanta was out of bread and milk and salt—out of a dozen things or more. Soon she would have to walk to the Messer farm, perhaps even the many miles to the next cove—or else live on nothing but the produce of the garden and the canned food in the pantry until it ran out. She hated the waiting, the fearing that Ba would not come, that Mama was gone forever. Always she had been a good, an obsessed reader, but now she forced herself to move her eyes along the weary lines of black that kept breaking into letters—meaningless sounds and shapes. Her mind would no longer bend to a book, to another realm. This world pressed onto her, pulling her attention to the window, the empty doorframe that no one ever filled, the landscape that stirred and burgeoned with the green of summer but never showed a human-like figure except the pale green shape of the spirit, growing in the maze. Even that made her feel uneasy, remembering Ba's stories of how Selu, the Corn Woman, was murdered; from her blood drops sprang the first corn. Still, she often felt that someone was watching her, and once she called out *Ba! Mama! Who's there?* to break the blank that was really no silence but made up of the songs of insects and birds. It frightened her, the noise of her own voice. Sometimes in the house she spoke in a whisper. It seemed to her that now and then she had to speak, if only to see if she still could.

For no one would be coming, no one would talk if she did not. There would be no meter reader, for after they moved to the cottage, Ba put in a generator and purchased kerosene lamps and candles for emergencies. Water came from the well or else from the mountain streams. Mama owned no other family; Adanta had never met any of her distant cousins, Ba's relatives, who lived somewhere off in the mountains, maybe as far as Tennessee. It seemed to her that she could die and no one would know, not for months or years. Ever since Ba had become ill, there had been no school for her except the sitting at the sunlit kitchen table, reading out loud or working math problems as her father sat watching or dozed in his chair. No, even before that—since the day he had showed them the Little Cottage and hurriedly moved their furniture and hastily packed boxes, as if he wanted to escape the world and hide. So no one would be expecting her in the next cove, not even when the end of August would arrive and the old school bell ring out, as it had done for more than a hundred years. If anyone asked, her teachers and classmates would say that she had moved, that she was home-schooled now.

As Adanta turned away from the mirror, the words of an old song came into her head: *Fly away home, my honey child; fly away home.*

She was home, she thought, yet not home. What was a house without parents? She had pored over photo albums, looking for clues, had examined every corner of every room—had learned nothing more about where her parents might be. She had sat behind the wheel of the old Chevy Apache, wondering if she dared to drive on the twisty mountain road. She had slipped her hands over the ranks of heavy Mason jars packed with the harvest of this and earlier years: peeled pears from trees behind the last house; peaches, with the tiny torch shapes of cloves floating in a gloom of syrup and sediment; seven kinds of peppers, from sweet to fiery; beans and summer squash and pumpkin and tomatoes. All had been prepared at home, Charlotte and Adanta working together around the canning pots, the pair of them perspiring and laughing, pleased with the bright containers of fruit and vegetables beside an open window. Adanta had broken one by leaving the tongs clamped on the jar, and it had cracked while cooling. Wordlessly the rows now spoke of summer days past but were mute about the ones to come. Where should she go? Nothing answered. Quiet was over all, the calm in the rooms blunting the noise of insect and stream and bird outside.

All the same, when she went to her closet and began to pack, it felt as if she knew where she was going, and she pulled out the basket with leather straps that had been a birth gift from her grandmother, according to Ba. It appeared as cunningly woven as a bird's nest, made from fine, tightly packed grasses and colored threads. Inside it she placed a few clothes, her mother's favorite knife—left behind on the window seat—some packages of rice cakes and dried fruit that were all the easy-to-carry food remaining in the house, and a comb.

Afterward she latched the front door and climbed out the window from which her mother had vanished. Tugging down the sash, Adanta glimpsed the room behind glass, looking as lifeless and untouchable as a roped-off parlor in a museum. She felt sure that this was the only way to start a search: to follow exactly the path she had seen her mother go. But where to proceed from there? She lacked direction and wanted to find out more, perhaps at the Messers' house. Reluctant to leave the Little Cottage, she perched on a rocky outcrop at the edge of the clearing, letting the wind tousle her hair, her face tilted to the warm sun. As she opened her eyes and glanced across the upper and lower fields, she caught a streak of color and rapid movement and stood up to see what was happening.

The Pony Boy, she whispered.

Sure enough, there was a dark-haired boy on horseback, galloping straight across one of the Messer fields. She hoped it was on the strips of grass that made roads between them, as the Messers were said to be hotheads, gigantic men with fierce tempers. It was not so strange that Adanta had never met any of their clan: her mother wouldn't allow it, even though they lived close by. One day she had seen a heavyset boy trudging along the dirt road, his wheelbarrow heaped with ginseng root that must have been dug from the place Jess called Sang Hollow. He could have been a Messer. At dawn she had heard a song sung with such volume and gusto that it seemed to drive the mists out of the vale. And once she had watched as a huge man—bearded with a black, bristling thicket—clambered up their hillside, a buck and a gun slung over one shoulder. Adanta believed every tall tale she had heard from Ba of their wildness, and she was sure that the big farmers wouldn't stand for a boy to go tearing up a field of corn or tobacco. *The Pony Boy*. She hadn't seen him in a long time.

When they had first come to the cove, she had spotted him frequently, riding along the fields, hallooing at the ravens and crows until they soared up—the birds unafraid but enjoying the back-and-forth scoffing with the boy. Then one afternoon he strayed into the upper fields. It was a day when Ba felt sick and weak, and Adanta had left the house because she did not want to listen to him speak in the frail, thin tone that sometimes made the tears, unbidden, spring to her eyes. She spied on the boy from the doorway, hidden by the spikes of cardinal flower that were now blooming wildly, extravagantly, the bright wicks flaring as high as her head.

He rode right up to the clearing, astride his sturdy splotched mustang. His eyes swept the newly painted cottage, now a muted yellow, and the repairs to the stone base, then paused at the planted-up garden, already as packed with leaves and flowers as though it had been growing there for many years.

"I swan, Polk," he said, scratching the pony's head, "the people are getting thick as bees in sourwood up in these coves."

Then he saw her behind the coarse green-and-red tapers and ventured along the edge of the lawn, staring at her.

"Hello," she ventured.

He nodded, sliding down from the horse's back. "What's your name?"

When she told him, he looked surprised.

"Adanta ain't—isn't a name for a person," he began, then added hastily, "but it's a very beautiful name. It's just that Adanta—Adantis is—" Here he broke off, staring dubiously at her.

"Do you live close by?"

No, he told her, waving one hand toward the west. He said that he lived farther back in the mountains. It had confused her at the time because there were no people beyond the government line. At least, there were none so far as she knew. Just as she was about to ask him, the boy, who had been examining her face carefully, broke out, "When I'm nineteen, maybe I'll come back and steal you away for my bride, and there'll be the biggest kind of party and feast anybody has ever seen in the hollers."

"You will not!" She turned to sprint into the house.

"Don't," he called out; "you can pet Polk, if you want to. It's just I forget—folks do things different in the Lands Beyond."

"Lands beyond what?" she said, confused again, but he didn't answer, pulling an apple from his pocket and handing it to her so that she could feed the pony.

She forgot to repeat *lands beyond what?* as she felt the breath on her hand, the muzzle softer than she would have imagined, the hard teeth. A froth of apple juice sluiced from the jaw as his head bent, searching in the grass for dropped fragments.

"Those green apples," the boy said, smiling, "they really pucker up your mouth." And this time he bent over and gave her a smacking kiss right on hers, so that she shoved him hard on the chest until he dropped down on one knee, laughing, wiping his eyes.

"I'm sorry," he said. "My mother would be all fretted to pieces if she saw me now. I really am sorry. You're just young," he added, which made her mad all over again.

"You can't be more than two or three years older—" she began.

"Listen." He held up one hand. "Would you like to ride on Polk with me? I could ask your folks. He's a half-Scottish horse—see that bump of bone on his forehead? It's a sign that he's part unicorn. That's what my father says, because in old times the Scottish King's sign was a unicorn."

Adanta started to shake her head, although her eyes darted to the little knob on the pony's brow.

"I won't steal you—never—nothing like that," he promised.

So at last she nodded, telling him that she thought it would be fine, that she didn't want to disturb her father, that he was sick. And when the boy looked sorry and asked about him, they sat in the grass for a time, the mustang snuffling at their pockets, and she told him all about Ba and Mama and how they had come to be living in the Little Cottage In Between. When he asked their names, the boy seemed surprised.

"That name I know," he said, referring to Ba. "And I think I've heard tell of parts where he grew up. At least the way to it. There's fearsome steep cliffs and wild woods, they say. I've been most places but not there—don't really even know the trails. Nobody much ever goes in that direction. Not on the road to anything, though it's not all that far off. I guess his mother must be pretty lonesome. Must live way up on the crags, if she's still alive."

"I don't think so," she told him. And never thought of it again until Mama mentioned Ba's mother, that perhaps she was luring him into the mountains, calling him from home.

What a lovely day it had been! The boy didn't let Polk gallop but picked a way down the sloping fields. The hot sun glinted on his perspiration and on the fine hairs on his bare back, and Adanta held him tightly by the waist until she grew confident, sitting up straight and moving with the pony's rhythm. They rocked past the upper fields, down into the lower ones, and at last reached the corn maze.

"It's a special kind of corn," the boy told her. "It always shoots up nine, ten feet tall. Course, the Messers grow pretty tall themselves. They've got a camp right near us—way up in the mountains. Nobody like a Messer for making cove juice. And nobody else is going to mess with a Messer. I swan, if they're not *Tsunil kalu* and juice men both."

Adanta leaned to one side and peered into his face.

He grinned back at her.

"Juice. Moonshine. You know what moonshine is, I reckon."

She knew. Ba had a little bottle in the cupboard, just for curiosity's sake. It was clear and thick, and something oily and rainbow-like but even more transparent was floating inside. The vapor had burned the inside of her nose when she sniffed at it. *And what was the other name he had called the Messers?*

"My folks would never fuss with such stuff," the

boy said. "My daddy is the best singer in all of Ad—in all the mountains. He wouldn't hurt his voice for all the sweet mash in the world. He is the best Teller of stories and the second-best mandolin-maker. And I mean to follow him."

Adanta didn't know what she wanted to do, except that she loved to read more than anything else.

"My parents have thousands of books," she said, telling him about how Ba had been a teacher and how Mama left shavings behind her wherever she went, even when her nose was poked in a novel.

He cast a look over his shoulder.

"Thousands of books? Nobody has thousands. I don't know anybody with a hundred, or even ten. Everybody has a Mooney. Everybody has the Bible. But that's it, unless maybe there's a baby's book with patch pictures."

"We do," Adanta said firmly. "And maybe I'll make books of my own when I grow up!" This popped out of her mouth before she thought, and surprised her. She paused, mulling over the idea, then asked, "What's a Mooney?"

"Mooney?" This time he twisted about in his seat, staring at her. "I swan. Your father comes from the backcountry mountains and you want to know,

What's a Mooney?" Turning around, he rubbed the pony's head.

They jogged along in a silence punctuated only by an occasional shuddering breath from Polk. It was a perfect August day, heat dancing in the distance and a breeze cooling the skin, and she could see clear across the cove—the atmosphere so crystalline that it seemed she could count the trees on the hills opposite. In the Messers' fields the beans and tobacco were in bloom, and bees and insects were hovering or zipping away across the cleared land, intent and busy.

Oh, and when they came to the Messer corn, she felt certain that there was nothing so tall and green in the world except a tree! The stalks towered up, dwarfing pony and rider. Inside the maze it was calm, the green leaves moving like ribbons in the current of air that filtered through the stems and the leaves beginning to rustle and remind her that fall was coming. It seemed that the Pony Boy already knew his way through the maze. That spring the paths had been cut into the shape of a great Uktena, a crowned river snake, coil upon coil under green waves of the corn leaves. The Pony Boy always knew where he was.

"Now we're in the belly of the snake," he would say, or, "Now we're in the crooked river weed under him. Now we're as far as the heart. The forking tongue."

The corn was an endless whispering, a soughing, a place of sighs. If she had gone by herself, she would have been afraid of the emptiness of the place, or else of stumbling upon one of the Messer men. *How big?* she had wondered. *High as the corn?*

The ride through the corn maze had been a long time ago. Nothing amazing about a girl wondering how tall a man might be, when corn grew so strangely lofty.

Now she was older. She remembered her face in the glass. It had looked different, the shadow wings of sleeplessness under her eyes, the cheeks thinner than before. Inside, she knew she was older. The days and the years would keep fluttering off, and year by year she would become a woman.

I do not want to grow up alone, she thought. *I am still a child—I forget that now, sometimes—but I am. I need Ba and Mama. I will find them, and I will bring them home.*

"If there is anything left to bring," she whispered.

Her glance followed the moving dot that was the Pony Boy. From here, her shout would only float away. That first summer he had come to see her three times, but on the third her mother had sent him away, waving vaguely at the mountains and saying, "I'm sorry. I don't want my daughter to know—someone from over there." Adanta could still picture his back, stiff and proud, riding off.

"Why, why did you do that?" she had cried out, spilling over with wrath.

"I'm sorry, Adanta," her mother had said. "It's just that everything is so unsettled here—and Ba—and this boy knows the Messers—they're not people we should be meeting." Her mother's hands had moved helplessly in the air.

"But he's not a Messer," Adanta had shouted. "He's not a Messer, and I liked him, really liked him. He's funny and different and he's—he's my one friend."

It had taken her days to stop being angry at her mother. The funny thing was, it seemed to her now, that when she was younger, she had never thought to learn his name. So that he was still only the Pony Boy, although the colt was Polk. He, too, would be older now, she remembered. What age had the boy been that August? She could no longer see him, so she stood up on the rock, shouldering her pack. There he was, dipping back into the maze. To catch

43

him, she would have to hurry. The Pony Boy might not come this way, even after so long a time—he would remember her mother's words. What had Mama meant by "over there"? Maybe she hadn't even known herself—maybe it was just that everything had been so uncertain after the move.

Adanta rubbed a hand lightly across her stomach. She was hungry, and right now she did not want to unseal another jar of squash or beans, or eat another dried apricot or apple. If she did not find him, she would dare the Messer lodge, a sprawling compound of log rooms and lean-tos hooked together by porches and dogtrots. The Messers were bound to be hungry women and men; there would be home-cooked food, and a lot of it.

Jumping to the grass, she headed down the slope, kicking stones and dirt on the steep places, easing off where the tilt lessened. She did not look back at the cottage with its blue window frames but kept her eyes on the maze, where the Corn Woman was no longer the tender green of spring but was day by day turning the deeper green of summer.

THE CORN MAZE

Adanta craned her neck to see above the tops of the corn, but it was impossible to make out the mountains that rose up blue until they met the morning clouds—nothing but a swath of sky showed high overhead. She could feel the world shifting a little, changing gears as she pushed into the cornfield. There was a hush in the maze; instead of the loud, complicated cry that was the voice of thousands of insects, there was a more delicate embroidery of sound, an orchestra of ticks and single held notes. Shreds of cloud snagged on the stalks and the ribbons of leaves, until a tickling faint breeze caught them up and pushed them on through the great sieve of corn. The field was a comb for the air, subduing the wind, dividing it into a thousand wayward curls. She had not remembered how green and shadowy the walls were, nor how still a realm the field could be when the wind died away. At once she forgot about the Pony Boy, although it had been only a few moments before that she had glimpsed Polk and his rider charge from the corn and then dive back. She had raced the last steps to the labyrinth, plunging inside without pausing to think about whether she might be afraid alone in the corkscrewing paths.

For an instant she had felt so, as crows slashed the air over her head and flew off cawing to another part of the field. After that fright, Adanta was fine, charmed by the secret leafy passageways. Wandering in one direction, then another, she let her worries drift away on the air until she had no thought for anything but the winding trails and the broad blades, rippling like an ocean.

"A maze of maize." She sighed, and let go all thought.

So calm, so peaceful was the spot that she hardly felt startled to realize that at some point she had begun following a raven. She could not remember when she had first seen the bird, nor when she had first searched after it—the bird lighting, stalking along the paths not like a fierce harrier of the air but like a creature more accustomed to a human presence. The raven seemed a bit comic, cocking its head, one eye rolling toward her, stopping to stab at a fat green worm, making a querulous *pr-r-uk* noise in its throat—a homey fowl, like a glossy black chicken.

She had forgotten to mark her way, and when the raven vanished, she stopped, wondering where she might be in all that greenness. Deep in the image of the Corn Woman, maybe.

Just then the Pony Boy thundered across a gap in the corn, not fifteen feet away from her. Adanta cried out, but he did not slow down. Probably he couldn't hear over the noise of Polk's hooves, thudding on the red clay.

The sound sank and died, and again she could hear the songs of katydids and cicadas. Adanta remembered stories about Mammoth Cave in Kentucky, how people who went wandering in its cave rooms and corridors could vanish, their bones never found. And yet in the old times many had been drawn to the caverns, to hide out or to explore. So, too, the living walls of the corn maze held a fascination. Which way to go? Her eye fell on a wavering snip of cloud. She bent and touched it; it was real, not mist as she first had thought. The yarn lay glistening on her palm, hardly more than a cobweb. Twirling the wisp around her finger, she discovered that it was no thrum but an actual thread, and followed its trail—walked along a straight pathway, zig-zagged back, then turned a corner and let out a sharp cry.

"Did I startle you? I didn't mean to frighten you."

The low breathy voice came from a figure, her knobby hands busy rolling the misty thread into a ball. When the woman raised her head, Adanta saw that she was quite elderly, perhaps the oldest person she had ever seen. Yet her hair was still dark except for a few streaks of white and, in fact, appeared to be the same auburn color as Adanta's. The brown eyes met her own. The girl was surprised to find that the old lady seemed scared; the crooked hands were trembling.

"You see, I was hoping you would come. Don't be afraid. I am your grandmother Birdie Ann—well, you may think of me as your great-grandmother, since I am so very ancient, if that seems easier. All your life I have wanted to meet you, and now that I do, I am glad to see that you look like me, a little, up close. And there—you are carrying my birth gift!" The old woman smiled at her. "That pack is a sign of what I am: a weaver, you see. Perhaps you will be like me in that, too. Perhaps you will be a weaver."

Birdie Ann was chattering, her voice quick, but as

Adanta stretched out a hand toward the fringed black shawl, she paused.

"Wait, wait," she cautioned. "I am very, very aged, as you can see. Don't even lay a finger on me. Sometime, someday. Are you well?"

Nodding, Adanta put out her hand again, but the other looked at her without smiling and did not take it.

"You don't look well. You don't look quite yourself. What about those black shadows under your eyes?"

Adanta was puzzled. *How did she know? Had she ever come to visit?*

"Oh, I've seen you many and many a time at the peep of day. Not so nigh as this. Antique as I am, I see far and clear, like a young eagle." The woman laughed, a cracked small cackle. "You and your ba and your dear mother, who was right not to trust me or want me around. Because she felt the shadow on me, dark and terrible. But I watch, because I have to—I cannot give up my Jess entirely, nor his child . . ." Here she shook her head, murmuring to herself.

"You see, I must not touch you or anyone else, not unless I'm sure you are well, with no sickness anywhere. Because I'm nothing but the most antiquated kind of a granny woman, because I am so terribly tottery and frail that the least thing might sweep me away—oh, I would be nothing but a bit of trash for the broom," she added, now smiling merrily. "Someday, though, when there is no darkness feathered under your eyes, I will rock you in my arms and be glad. Yes," she went on, again appearing to talk to herself, "there will come a day when we can hold each other and not be afraid."

The old lady busied herself with the ball, which she tucked away into a pocket under her voluminous shawl, before turning to feed a campfire with sticks. A pot on the fire sent up a steam that smelled fragrant to the girl, who had not eaten a hot meal for many days.

"I am hungry," she ventured.

"That's good. It's fine to be hungry and to have a relish for your dinner. But you must be careful not to take food from strangers, you see, after this—you see?"

"What do you mean?"

"Just that if you are unsure about someone, do not eat."

Adanta stared at the grandmother without answering.

Clapping her hands, the woman exclaimed, "I hardly ever dine anymore. I'm so old that I can live without food. The air itself is almost too rich for me." She winked, gesturing for the girl to sit. "But a grandmother likes to feed her family. That's why I am cooking, because I knew you might be coming."

"Grandmother, you watched us. Do you know where Ba is?" And Adanta told her the whole story of Ba's quest for the healing lake, and about the Lean One and his coming to take her mother away.

While her granddaughter talked, the old woman dished up a bowl of corn mush, as it proved to be. The girl ate it eagerly, pausing now and then in her tale to shovel the warm corn into her mouth. Her relative, if so she was, listened quietly, nodding half-sleepily from where she sat hunched in her shawl. Adanta was not sure she was following the whole story, but when she was done, the grandmother tilted her head to one side, looking at Adanta with shining eyes.

"I have seen Jess," she said.

"Ba—"

"It was some weeks ago. I believe you will see him, too, but whether he will come home again I do not know. He was injured in a quarrel; that's all he would tell me. And he did not have on blue flannel, as you describe," she added slowly. "He wore a filthy rag of a shirt, and so I gave him another of my own weaving, a white one meant for my husband. For that, Kalanu was angry and gave me hard words."

"Ba," Adanta repeated. She wondered if the old woman knew more than she was saying.

"By now Jess is farther west, still searching for the healing lake. He sent me to spy on you and your mother, and now it seems she has fallen prey to some love charm, perhaps to a wizard, perhaps to one of the Raven Mockers."

"My mother doesn't believe—"

"By now, she might."

The grandmother bent over the fire, sprinkling it with dirt, and when she spoke again, there was a trace of bitterness in her voice.

"Their kind has been the ruin of more than one young woman."

Here, by one of those odd coincidences that always startle, a silent raven skated by, just above the tops of the corn, for a moment casting his shadow on the grandmother's lap.

She jumped up from her seat, saying, "I don't know what I was thinking, staying so long. My husband will beat me. He is old—old and crotchety. Changed from what he was. He loved me once; he stole me from my parents, in the Adantan way, but I wouldn't give him all that he desired, wouldn't be like him—only once, and that by trickery."

Adanta reached out a hand, confused by her words.

"Great-grandmother, please don't go—stay with me—and what is the Adantan way? *I* am Adanta."

"Call me Grandmother, Adanta. It is shorter, easier. As for your own name, Jess named you as he wished. Now, listen. I must go, and I must go soon. I thought this spot would be secret, but now I am afraid—"

"But there's no one to see, nothing but birds and bugs—"

The old woman winked and said, "Even the Corn Woman has ears." Clasping her shawl close, she bent forward, lowering her voice. "There are more things to tell you—Adantis is what we call our lands to the west, the lands where the settlers and the Cherokee lived together and intermarried, those who would not live in places with roads and towns, who could not bear to see the body of the mountains cut and torn for gain. For greed. Back then the whole land was God's country. Now in many places it is maimed and ugly and belongs only to men. Hush—don't speak. There is no time," she told Adanta. "I can't say more, but I will see you again. Maybe I can draw you to me, as I did today, if you come near. Do not go to the towns in the Lands Beyond. Go westward, and you may help Jess and your mother. In Adantis, those who are good are kind to children. The others you will know as you knew the Lean One.

"I must fly—must run home. But I have three gifts for you, which will help on your trek."

Adanta's grandmother fished about beneath her shawl, looking for a package. She seemed to have a large number of parcels and bags stored about her body, and it was some moments before she cried *"Ah!"* and drew something small and shining from a pocket. Carefully she unknotted the object, shaking out a glistening fabric, which she cast over the girl's shoulders. Lifting her arms outward, Adanta wondered at the many shades of green, shot through by dazzling streaks. The weaving reminded her a little of a spider's web, so delicate was the pattern, so fine the thread.

Adanta twirled, the cloth flying about her body like a cape. When she stopped, it hung downward in silken folds, glittering with rainbow colors like a pair of insect wings. As in a magic trick, the cloth could be wound about her body like a green cocoon or, thin and airy, it could be pulled through the grandmother's ring, or yet again be folded smaller, small—then knotted by two small strings sewn to the outer edge.

"The stole will keep you safe and warm in all weather, no matter where you sleep," her grandmother said hurriedly, continuing to search under her shawl.

This time she pulled out and tossed an amulet, a small woven bag, for which she claimed protective powers. Adanta knew her mother would not have approved of such a thing, but she caught and turned the tiny sack in her hands, unwilling to reject any gift her grandmother might have to offer. The bag was woven from mulberry-dyed thread and fastened to a necklace of braided green. Loosening the gathering string, she peeped inside.

"What is it?"

"Don't touch!" The old woman reached toward the girl, then drew back. "There's a strip of skin shed from an Uktena, which I found snagged on a laurel branch. The curled thread is a hair from the head of one of the Little People. The folded paper—it has the sacred names of God written on a page corner torn from the Bible." She lowered her voice. "And the downy feather? Stolen from a Raven Mocker's breast.

"Don't ask me how I got it," the grandmother whispered, looking frightened.

"But Raven Mockers are—"

"Ba's fairy tales? Stories? Be careful, child. Don't refuse my gift."

Adanta looped the necklace around her neck, touching the braided thread with one finger. Whether it would help or not, it was curious to behold, the workmanship very fine. Her grandmother was surely a famous weaver.

The third gift was a journal of blank pages, the cover woven from many-colored threads. It showed a picture of the Little Cottage In Between, the house and garden with its bees, a curtain with the shadow of a bent head. The paper was clearly made by hand, flecked with marks that looked almost like the start of words—as if words and worlds were already trying to surface. Adanta remembered what the Pony Boy had said, that in Adantis there were only two volumes, the Bible and Mooney. When she had asked Ba about Mooney, her mother had become upset, and Ba had not answered, only saying that he had gotten rid of his copy "to please your mother."

"It is not our way in Adantis, but it is your way, the way of print. For a time it was also mine. In my loneliness and unhappiness I was once a great reader of stories from the Lands Beyond. That was while Kalanu still loved me; later, when he was sure I would never care for him, he burned my books. He had given them; he took them away. After that I wove my thoughts on the loom. So this seemed good to me. What use you make of it—that is up to you."

The grandmother glanced up at the sky.

"If I am to be home in time, I must leave. I cannot stay longer, but there is so much you do not grasp . . ."

She sighed, her eyes on Adanta's face.

"I don't know. In Adantis, the innocent may well find a road that others do not."

Feather-light gladness brushed Adanta, the necklace safe around her neck, the journal and cloth in her hands. When she tried to embrace her grandmother, the old woman cried out, "I cannot! I must go!" and whirled about, darting with surprising speed into an opening in the maze.

"Grandmother, no!" Adanta called, "Come back— wait for me!" The girl let the gifts tumble to the ground as she rushed after her grandmother, then stopped. Past the gap in the corn lay seven or eight possible ways to go, with no one in sight. She cast a glance over her shoulder, then slowly walked back to the smothered fire, letting her woven basket down from her shoulders. Inside it she placed the stole, the book, and the few things her grandmother had left behind: a sack of coarsely ground corn, a pot freshly scrubbed with sand, a spoon, a wooden bowl, a box of kitchen matches. Untying a knotted rag, she found seven gold coins. Three of them showed a Liberty head that was not a woman's face but the narrow, bold, and sinewy face of a man. The others were stamped with a brooding female profile and the name *Agawela*. On the reverse side, some of the coins showed a scene of tents and pennants, others a windowless log cabin. The word ADANTIS arced in the sky overhead. They were true coins, rough and crude at the edges but with the solid heft of the real. Adantis, then, must be genuine, too, with its own exchange of money, laws, customs . . . But how to get there?

"I will," Adanta said out loud. *Not the roundabout twenty miles by dirt road to the village. Not that. Due west to Adantis.*

Seeing a line of floating floss like a spider's thread fastened to a cornstalk, she followed its shining filament, and, as if provided by the grandmother, it led her out of the labyrinth. There were her familiar mountains, now with the clouds lifted from their heads, and there the upper fields and barns of the

Messer farm and the lower fields and woods in the valley below. All looked new and fresh to her eyes, although she had seen the cove a thousand times before. Then, heralded by a puff of dust, the Pony Boy on Polk galloped from the far end of the maze.

"Wait," Adanta shouted, but in an instant more the horse and rider plunged into the forest and were gone.

Magpie Joe

The Messer yard was like no place Adanta had been. A rope lay in loose scribbles across the clearing where a worn-out wagon, some adzed logs, a hobbyhorse big enough for a half-grown boy, and an abandoned basket spilling over with laundry served as nesting spots for a brood of beady-eyed chickens. Brassy-yellow and bold as only the addle- and feather-brained can be, they scuttled across the yard, bobbing their heads and pecking around Adanta's legs.

"Shoo, shoo," she ordered, shoving them aside with her feet, but they paid no mind. Up close, the Messer house was monumental, a series of great pens made from timbers still so at home in the forest that here and there a green shoot was seen, rooted in the mud chinking between logs. The split shingles on the roof were velvety, padded with moss. Adanta squatted to squint under the house, where the crawl space beneath was rank with the smell of hound dogs—only one old fellow snored in the shade, his eyelids and front legs trembling, a paw lapped over a bone. The compound felt empty, the great stalls for the Messers' Clydesdales yawning open, and not a child at play or a grown Messer at work was to be seen. Cautious, ready to jump and flee down into the valley like a bolting squirrel, Adanta climbed onto a sagging porch and peered past a half-open door.

"Hello," she called. "Are you all home? Hey, anybody?" Her voice trailed off as she pushed back the thick slab of wood.

There was no answer, and following the lead of a chicken, she stepped in.

No fresh-cooked feasts here, she thought, even if the Messers *were* home. The room was surely a kitchen, although with nothing much to show its purpose except a green pump at a soapstone sink and a big greasy woodstove. A cup lay on its side by the doorsill, its bowl as deep as a child's pail.

Big.

Her eyes flashed around the room, taking in the hubcap-sized plates on a shelf, a stinking trencher of meat spotted with flies, the broken chair in a corner.

She could almost hear Mama's voice saying, "Sheer fecklessness." The Messers had just up and abandoned fields and dishes, dogs and chickens. Uneasy, she jumped when a mouse skittered from behind the stove and ran squeaking along the wall.

Where had they gone?

Not sure whether to be glad or sorry, she relaxed, looking curiously around the room. Opposite the sink a single wide door hung ajar, giving notice of a family cupboard stored with gallon canning jugs of beans, squash, and tomatoes. On the bottom shelf, a speckled fowl clucked and shifted on her nest, warning Adanta that serious efforts were in progress. When the girl swept the hen from her perch with a broom, she turned out to have been trying to hatch an empty saltshaker. Only on the high table was there what looked like edible food—a cottage loaf, about the size of the hassock parked in front of her mother's favorite armchair at home. It looked crusty and brown, but when Adanta touched it, she saw that it was stale and as hard as a stone, impossible to dent. Like feather bolsters fired from catapults, three chickens flapped upward in a short cackling flight and, landing near the loaf, gave it a goggle-eyed inspection. They pecked at it without much enthusiasm, chipping off a few slivers before losing interest entirely. When the three hopped down and wandered off into a farther room as if accustomed to forays inside the house, Adanta watched them disappear in the shadows.

What was it about chickens? she wondered, wishing that she could tell Ba about how the hens had gossiped over the loaf before taking a stab. *So funny-looking.*

First casting a quick glance into the darkness beyond the kitchen, where she could see a large stiff chair like a throne in the gloom, Adanta fled back to the porch. This time she saw a tattered note stuck to a nail: *Harlan Messer do you com. We-uns be a-goin west to the sumer plase and fair so com.*

That didn't sound so fearsome; in fact, it wasn't much different from how plenty of the children up in the coves spoke. The Messers had traveled west, though, into the wild lands, into what she now knew must be Adantis.

Well, Adanta concluded, soon she would be crossing over into that country, too, whatever it was, and she would just have to hope that her pack of food held out until she found Adantans—the Hidden People, the Pony Boy had said. She trusted they were not too good at hiding, for her ground corn and dried fruit and rice cakes would not keep her long.

Maybe she would find the Messers' camp, their "sumer plase," in Adantis.

The Messers didn't seem so frightful now that she had seen their rambling house, though they were no doubt large and definitely sloppy. There was nothing evil here. Of course they would feed her, should she find them. What silly thoughts she had had—that the Messers were wild giants, cannibals, ogres . . .

It was hard to believe such things in the sunny clearing, hard to remember the old frights. Yet in the mountains a walker's mood can change swiftly as she travels from the inhabited coves to those where for miles there is nothing alive to see but the deer floating out from the trees to feed in the dusky meadows. The change in altitude from the warm valley to the heights, often dank with blowing clouds, can sweeten or chill a mood. Adanta crossed the Messers' weedy yard, where the hound dog now lay with his white paws in the air. The rest of the chickens were nowhere to be seen.

Probably perched all over some overstuffed chairs, Adanta thought, imagining the hens sprinkled about an old-fashioned parlor, each one on a doily. It occurred to her that perhaps the Messers didn't have doilies or even chairs, that more than likely they squatted around one of the big chimneys that rose up from each set of rooms—stones at the bottom but built of sticks and mud at the top, like a caddis fly's case. She pictured them gnawing on bones, occasionally throwing one to a hound. The firelight cast a dancing gold on their faces . . . although she could not make up her mind whether they should look like the cave people in Ba's *Natural History Encyclopaedia*, with their crude, flattened faces, or whether they might be quite ordinary, or yet again surprisingly beautiful.

All the time she went on daydreaming about the absent Messers, her feet kept on taking her out of the yard, down along the Corn Woman's side, and into the valley. It was farther than she had realized, and after the first half hour she longed for the Pony Boy to appear and give her a ride up the hills and into the mountains. By the time the sun burned in the very top of the sky, Adanta was weary of walking, but she kept on. Though it was hours until dark, she might have to go many more up-and-down miles before reaching a house in Adantis. There she would find her father's people; they were good to children, her grandmother had said. If they were not, she would turn and run for it, losing herself in a laurel thicket. At last the ground began to rise underfoot, and she was climbing even before she realized that she had come to the end of the valley. Sweaty, thirsty, she scaled the high hill, then sat on a boulder at the top, surveying the range on range of mountains beyond. It was daunting to see, a perfect image of endlessness. For the first time she turned to look back. There was the cove of home, with a pale green patch that must be the Corn Woman asleep in her maze and beyond it a spark of burning brightness that must be the metal top of the Little Cottage In Between shining in the sun. As she stared at the single point of light, she wished that she could go back and find Ba reading at the kitchen table, her mother digging in the garden—that the only clouds in her days were the ones ripe with the summer rains that drummed so pleasantly on the tin roof of home.

As with all wishes that flare up like a sunset, this one faded away, doubtless to return another time in all its vivid colors.

Shouldering her pack, Adanta began the descent into the next cove, picking her steps along rough ground. Beaten tracks, faint worn lines of earth, scrambled here and there on the slope, but on the valley floor she found sure footing. Trails crisscrossed the earth; this was clearly not the wild land that her grandmother and the Pony Boy had described. By dusk she had made it to the far side of the valley, where the mountains soared up higher than she had envisioned when standing on the hill-tops of her home cove.

Here she felt afraid, seeing that the sun would flicker and fall behind the edge of the mountain be-fore she could find a house, a place to stay. Never had she slept out in the wild without a shelter, nor had she ever thought to hike alone. She had often camped near the booths of craft fairs with her par-ents; while Mama set up her displays, Adanta would shout and play with other children, and Ba would wander the aisles of wares, coming back with strange trinkets and stories of his adventures. Even after the retreat to the Little Cottage, Jess was willing to load the Apache with boxes of carvings, lash a tarp over all, and take off—if well enough to go, he relished any kind of fair, and he liked sleeping under the stars, although his wife did not. Charlotte liked to loll in the rippling grass, talking and laughing and picking out the constellations, but afterward she wanted to curl up inside the tent, safe under the fly that kept off dew and rain, behind the mesh doors that zipped against bites and stings. How frightened she would have been to think of her daughter ram-bling without a guide! Mama had warned her about boys and girls who wandered off in the soil, never to reappear. There were sinkholes in the forest, places where the wilderness was unsteady, where underground streams had hollowed caves or where a long-rotten stump and its unseen roots could collapse and bury a child. Those things were more of what Charlotte had feared. Adanta shook her head. It could not be common. Or if so, then she would just have to take that risk. She thought of her father's sparkleberry staff, a twisted limb with mingled pale and cinnamon colors, the light floating shapes like clouds on the darker wood. Tomorrow she would cut a branch with her mother's knife; that way she could test the ground as she walked. So far the world seemed solid enough.

Remembering the blade made her jump up and fish it from the bottom of the pack where it had sunk, a small solid object. It was not much of a weapon of defense but better than none at all. Inspecting the ground nearby, she chose a spot close to a stream and soft with leaf litter, then tore branches from a balsam tree and piled them on the ground. It would have to do. But she was hungry. Gathering dry brush, she built a tepee of sticks and used three of her precious matches to start a fire. That went pretty well, thanks to Ba's past care in teaching her how to make a safe, warm camp, but it was a very long time before the mountain water grew hot enough to cook some of the corn from her grandmother's sack. Then it was chilly and dark—darker than she had ever imagined the world could be. The walls of the mountains blotted out any light until, despite the mist and clouds, the roof of sky began, star by star, to shine and cast its radiance on the valley. Oh, she was not so afraid of a bear as of something worse—whatever it was that made the branches saw together and the twigs snap. Or perhaps it was the vastness of the landscape that felt so alarming. At night the mountains seemed larger than ever. As she began wolfing down the corn mush, the top of the moon glinted over the edge of the ridge. By its gleam she hung her pack in the trees, scrambling up a few feet before looping the straps over a bough far too small to hold a bear. Hoping to prevent the odor of food from drawing animals, she washed the spoon and left the empty pot to soak in the fast-running stream.

The stole, knotted up small, lay on her palm.

Carefully untying the strings, she shook it out. In the firelight it appeared not so much green as the deep blue of twilight, shot through by the shining rays of stars. Cocooning the fabric around her body, she lay down on the bed of fir and looked up at the moon in its halo. The stole was surprisingly roomy and warm, its softness consoling, calming. It made a kind of refuge. She stretched the cloth out, tucking it over her feet and pulling a piece across her face. Then for a moment she was startled, hearing the faint *whoosh* of a bird landing in the balsam trees. Although she had been sure that she was too restless to fall asleep, it seemed that sleep was waiting for her, and in an instant she plunged into its dreamless depths.

At dawn she woke, dewdrops dripping from the ends of the stole onto her eyelids. After breakfasting on dried fruit, she once again started to climb, but this day her legs were sore and painful. Travel was hard, even with the help of a fresh-cut hickory staff. Not until she had been trudging upward for some time did she feel better. It was the same the following morning after another night out in the open. However, by the next day, after a few hours of tramping across another valley, she was surprised to find that she was walking faster and more energetically than she had before. The ruts and trails had nearly vanished, and she was hiking down an almost dry streambed, hopping from stone to stone, when she caught a snatch of sound—what she thought to be the first human voice that she had heard since her mother had slipped from the blue-painted windowsill and said, "It's fine." No, she remembered; there was the grandmother in the corn maze, with her hasty advice and her gifts. It seemed long ago.

She craned her head, looking to each side of the channel, but saw nothing. After leaping onto the bank, she pushed through a grove of trees into a brushy ravine, where she stood listening, head cocked.

There it was, a faint noise of singing . . .

And sure enough, deep in the undergrowth, bobbing along as though he might be bouncing on his toes, was a man in a gray coat of peculiar cut. He wore a cap of bluish velvet, sewn all over with bits of silvery trash, strips of foil and tin and jingle bells. Likewise his twisted staff was topped with a shower of bells and bright ribbons. Adanta waded into the scrub, breaking off branches in her pell-mell rush after the fellow.

He couldn't hear her call over the sound of his own nasal voice:

The crow-in-the-moon, he married a girl,
  With a flippety, pippety fla pa la,
She wore a fine ring of diamond and pearl,
  With a flitterly, pitterly la la fah.
She lay in the bed till broad sunny day,
  With a westerly, nesterly la na la—

Here Adanta, panting at the man's heels, managed to brush his sleeve with her hand, making some of the tiny bells, sewn here and there on his coat, ring out.

"Oh," he cried, jumping sideways and flailing at the air, "a child, is it? Have you been following me? What do you want?"

"No, I—"

"Doesn't matter, doesn't matter: just a chick. She gave me the all-overs, the fine quick shivers, didn't she? Gave me quite a shock. Indeed she did, indeed she did, my dears." He nodded vigorously, patting his sides up and down as if he were searching for a lost wallet.

Swiftly trailing the man, Adanta cast a look over her shoulder, with a sudden thought that they might not be alone, but there was no one else: nothing but green leaves.

"Howsomever the little female thing crept up to my side, who can say," he muttered, "when I was swinging along, quite happy?"

"I'm sorry if I scared you," she called, trotting faster to keep up with his swift pace.

"Scare me? It would take somewhat more than a child to frighten *me*," the man declared, drawing himself up. "And that nothing but a girl child as well," he said as if to himself. "It's this terrible botheration and plague of the women, isn't it?" At this he broke into a gallop, his outer garment flapping as if he might open it wide and lurch upward, making a graceless, heavy burst into the air. This odd appearance was made even stronger by the design of the coat, which fell into two great curves at the hem, with a split sewn at the back, almost to his neck.

He looks like one of the Messers' chickens, Adanta thought, pounding along behind him. *Or no—something darker—a crow.* He stumbled and bounded faster, so that she had to redouble her efforts to keep up. Then, abruptly, he jerked to a stop and kneeled down, touching his forehead to the earth three times.

"Ahhh," he sighed, drawing out a big feathery fan and cooling himself with it, "that's ever so much better. Isn't it? I didn't mean to get so—so carried away with myself."

Adanta noticed that the strange man now stood flat on his feet and that when he stepped off again, he moved more normally. In addition, he seemed friendlier, turning to glance at her, so that she got a fine look at his uncommonly long nose, his eyes that were as black and shiny as new buttons, and his sleek black hair, streaked with gray.

"Dear poor child," he said, as if beginning a tête-à-tête.

It was on the very tip of her tongue to say, "I'm not your dear, and I'm not poor, and furthermore—" when he beamed right into her face.

"*Forgive* me," he sang, doling out another big, loopy smile. "It's my profession, you see. A constant danger to me, it is. When I start to get lifted right off my toes, when I feel all fluttery and in ill sorts, or when I get to sniping at the women, then I know it's high time for me to go to ground. It's all linked up with my profession," he confessed cheerfully, again patting down his coat. "They have too much influence on me. Draw me right off terra firma if I'm not careful. And they don't all of them like my wife, you see," he added in a whisper. "She's a good deal too clean and orderly. Puts them in her cages, hangs them out in the dogtrot at home, and they don't like that, they don't. It's good for their health, it is, but what do they care? They don't mind being free in the house; they'd stay there and like it. But she can't stand having the wee dirty footprints on all our doilies and antimacassars and such. Severe, she is, about soil."

He paused, fanning himself.

"What," Adanta asked, trying to catch her breath, "whatever do you mean?" Which itself sounded like a question he would ask, and not like her own words at all.

"Oh, oh," the long-nosed man lamented, "oh, dear, dear, dear. It's a terrible habit I have of beginning everything all skimble-scamble, the wrong way round. And then of course, it's impossible to go back to the start—"

"Why?" Adanta asked.

Removing a pair of wire-rimmed spectacles from the breast pocket of his shirt, he perched them on the very tip of his nose and peered at her.

"Why, indeed?" he murmured. "What an intelligent egg-chick it is. A preternaturally intelligent child."

The girl was unsure about whether she liked being called *a preternaturally intelligent child*, but she kept quiet, watching as the man screwed up his mouth and gave the distinct appearance of a person engaged in the effort of thinking. After a stretch of slow pacing, in which Adanta entirely recovered her breath and began to wish for something to eat and to wonder whether "egg-chick" might not be an insult, he bowed.

"Magpie Joe, at your service, purveyor of fine trained birds, imported and local, black-and-white talking magpies, nightjars, finches, ravens, crows, Scots rooks, pigeons for bearing messages, and mountain snowbirds."

"Adanta," she replied, afterward adding "at your service" and "child." She dipped slightly, imagining that a curtsy should answer a bow, even in the heart of the forest.

"My birds are all good creatures," he said with pride, "most locally hatched, even the Scots ones. Their great-great (ever-so-many-greats) grandparents were toted over by one of mine, sailing out of Solway Firth in the year 1774 anno domino." Here, while Adanta was puzzling over his error, he flung back the two wings of his strange costume to show a great many pockets of different sizes, each with a bird tucked inside, a short velvet cap tied over its beak.

It was Adanta's turn now to exclaim and express how he had surprised her, while he bowed again, smiling with sheerest delight.

She leaned forward, her glance taking in the pocketed birds, the glittering dark eyes and the shut lids like minute shells. She pored over each in turn, admiring them and wondering over the tiny velvet muzzles.

"I am glad, very glad," Magpie Joe murmured, closing the curtains on his birds. "And now, unless you have need for one of my fowl—Adantan coin only, no scrip—nothing but the true silveren or gold skirlings—I must be going." And without a stop for goodbye, he began trotting rapidly away.

"Wait," Adanta cried, chasing after him again; "please wait."

Shaking his head, he tossed another smile at her.

"Can't, indeed, or I'll be late as usual."

"Late for what?" she called, falling behind a little.

Magpie Joe looked rearward at her in astonishment.

"What*ever* is the world coming to?" he wondered, slowing until Adanta could catch up. "Why, tardy getting back to the Pony Fair, of course—only the best fair of the whole year, with booths and tents and the people from far and near to buy fairings and goods and horses. Not to mention proper featherings for girls." Here his glance lit on her blue jeans. "There are tents for moonshine whiskey and grits, or

78

griddle cakes or gigged-frogs-on-a-stick. It used to be shine-and-sugar for the babies and children, but now we're beyond the old ways—there's a man who comes with his fruit press, and often there's crushed cherries mixed with water-and-honey to drink. What part of Adantis are you from, not to know the Pony Fair? Why, even the horse robber bands roam about there quite freely, drinking and going at each other, rough and tumble. There's those who don't mind *buying* from a pony thief, but nobody likes robbers hanging around his own stock. Oh, the people are wild for the fair, for the games and the shooting at marks, and the contests for the best hand at a fiddle, the best at jumping or throwing a tomahawk and so on. My wife, Caledonia," he confided, "my own wife, Caledonia, is the best turkey caller in the land, and she can bring in hog or dog quicker than most."

What part of Adantis *was* she from?

Adanta hesitated, considering whether to tell Magpie Joe her story, but before she could begin, the two started climbing again.

"It's not far from here," he panted; "best to save your breath."

"May I go?" she asked, struggling to keep up with him. Her legs felt wobbly, but she could not stop to eat. She would just have to push on, no matter what.

Besides, the dried fruit had been gone since morning.

Magpie Joe paid no attention until she repeated the question.

"May you go?" he scoffed. "Who can't go? Who doesn't go? Of course you may go. And look at you—you're going already. Just don't expect me to slow down on the slidy rock and cliffs for a mere twittering chick." With this, he shut his mouth and began to climb faster. Adanta noticed that he was beginning to bob again as he walked and that he cocked his head one way, then another as he looked about him for a good path upward. She breathed through her nose, trying not to gasp for air. She would keep up with the bird peddler, and she would go to the Pony Fair, where there might be someone who knew her father or mother or the Lean One. When they stopped, she would ask him, and she would question his wife, Caledonia. If she was so good at calling animals, maybe she would know a way to call a man or a woman—or to call a Raven Mocker. If the Lean One was a Raven Mocker.

"Females," Magpie Joe groaned.

Adanta held well back from him on the steep slope, afraid his temper was rising.

Flighty. That's what he is.

For a while she could hear him muttering; then suddenly he pitched forward and pressed his forehead against the ground three times.

"That's better," Magpie Joe said, plumping himself down with his coat spread around him. As he waited for Adanta to catch up, a slow smile widened on his face. "You must be starved. Let's perch a minute. How about the last crumbs of Caledonia's cold johnnycake and a smidgen of sweet potato?"

THE PONY FAIR

Just before the track swerved into a deep dell, Magpie Joe, who had been fluttering along the trail with arms extended and the wings of his coat up-lifted, fell to his knees and once again knocked his forehead three times against the earth. The final time he left it there, and when Adanta caught up with him, he was still head down, his coat flung open so that she could see the winking eyes of the birds glittering from his pockets. When he at last lifted his face, he looked exhausted, his sallow complexion even paler than before. A smile, beginning with a faint tug at one corner, crept across his face. There was a smear of red clay on his brow. Adanta looked at the dirt but said nothing. Perhaps it would help keep his mind and feet on the ground.

"Tra lee, tra la, dear child," he caroled, snuffing

up the breeze with his big nose, "I scent the odorous airs of the Pony Fair. Delightful! And where there is the Pony Fair, there is Caledonia, waiting for me." He closed his eyes. "Griddle and pot on the fire, too, hissing and bubbling for Magpie Joe. And for you, dear child." Carefully he opened his coat and inspected his wares, stroking the head of a restless bird and tucking a wing back into a pocket.

Sniffing, Adanta took in the smell of damp earth and manure and something else—hot grease, perhaps. It made her stomach give out a weak growl of protest at its own near emptiness, not at all sated by the recent picnic.

"Ah, Cal, Cal, Cale-donia, donia," the peddler trilled, beginning to skip. "Sweet Caledonia, round and rubicund Caledonia."

Not sure what *rubicund* Caledonia might mean, Adanta followed his skipping feet.

"Rare as a ruby and apple-cheeked," he sang.

So it was red, rosy as a ruby, she guessed, beginning to skip at the thought of hot food. It was lovely, skipping. She promised herself that when she was entirely grown, she would keep on skipping—no matter if she looked as peculiar as Magpie Joe, joggling along with a dab of mud on his forehead.

When they rounded the last curve of path, Adanta

cried out with pleasure. Below her rippled the pennants and banners of the Pony Fair, flying above a motley collection of tents. Some appeared shaggy, some smooth, stitched from scraped animal hides. Some were dyed and woven and resembled so many colorful hats tossed into a ring. As she drew closer, hard on the heels of Magpie Joe, she could see that the circle of tents was larger than it had looked at first sight and that it was crisscrossed by grassy, wandering lanes. A few windowless cabins stood among the tents. A long-haired man with a cudgel spat tobacco in their direction and sang out, " 'Lo, Joe."

Magpie Joe's face cracked into a fresh smile.

" 'Lo, Cucumber. How's the fair been today?" He looked at the cudgel. "Had to knock some heads?"

"Three or four. It's a good'un yet. There's been a regular hellabaloo since sunup. The Messers came through with their horses and moonshine and made the biggest kind of a ruckus. Then again, that's what they do every morning."

Adanta stood in the shadow of Magpie Joe's coat, wondering what kind of *good* was meant.

"What you got there?" asked the man Magpie Joe had called Cucumber.

"Nothing so very much. Just the usual. And this thing—a girl nobody's ever seen before."

"Against the laws to bring in foreigners," Cucumber observed, pitching his cudgel from hand to hand. "Not that I'd stop you, but some might. It's a hell-roaring bunch, this crowd is."

"The poor nestling is hungry. I found it in the woods," the bird peddler said, then added, "or I suppose it found me."

"I belong here," Adanta said firmly, putting her trembling hands behind her back. She told them her father's name, told them about her grandmother Birdie Ann.

"That's right familiar," Cucumber told Magpie Joe. "There was a weaver lady with that name. Lived up in the laurel some time back. Seven or eight miles west of here. People said she sure had a mean old man—used to scare travelers."

Seven or eight miles west of the Pony Fair. She stored the information away. After all, hadn't her grandmother said, *I will see you again?* But how had her grandmother come so far, and how had she gotten back in time for supper? Maybe the old woman was a little mad.

A burly man dressed in homespun overshirt and trousers pushed forward, followed by a straggle of little children.

"So there you be, Joseph," he called. "Caledonia

has been fretting, a-waiting on you to come all the day long."

His offspring stared, their eyes wide and shiny, unblinking. Two dirty-faced boys were clamped to their father's shirttail, while the three girls clustered behind them, peeping out at Adanta. They were wearing coarse-woven dresses with shawls knotted around their necks. One of them wore boots with the buttons half off, but the others were barefoot.

"Flock of urchins," said Magpie Joe in a despairing tone, nodding to the father.

"Show us your hawkses, mister," one of the little boys begged, and then there was a chorus of "Please, Mister Joe" and cries of "Give us a penny."

"No birds, no birds today," he replied, digging in his pockets and flinging a few coins into a patch of dog-hobble, whereupon the whole group squealed and scattered, hunting in the leaves.

"Come on," Magpie Joe said to Adanta, "let's flit."

Indeed, he did seem to fly down the narrow alleys of the tent village, now and then perching on a box or stump to sweep his eyes over the tent tops. He fed her scraps of information along the way, saying, "There's a revival tent . . . They handle snakes, rattlers and copperheads, and speak in tongues . . . That's Black Betty's shine stall, the one with the copper pipe holding up the red banner, and there's another . . . That booth all shiny with beads is where they'll make a belt or jewelry . . . There's the white-weaver; nothing but flax there, traded with out-landers, and you could get you some proper dress . . . If you like frog legs, that's a gigger's shop, the one with the skinned frogs-on-a-stick around the door . . . The cobbler there makes wooden lasts and shoes . . . See the flag that's a copperhead skin? That's a witch-master, the one who cures witch-spell sicknesses and sells cats' bones and snakes' rattles and April Fool's rainwater and such, for spells and charms . . . There's another one, there with the shock of green corn by the tent flap, but he's a farmer's witchmaster, helps with planting by the zodiac . . . and the blood purifier, she's there in the reddish tent with the bunch of dried Dutchman's-breeches pinned to the door . . . and the Holy Fire Sanctification revival tent . . . a Storyteller of animal myths in the fur tent, a History Teller there, in the bark shed, and a well-known Teller of the Terrible and Sacred Myths there, in one of those Cherokee-style log houses that stays after the tents are gone and the bark houses are falling to pieces."

Three times during this headlong account of the Pony Fair, Magpie Joe halted to tap his forehead on soil, each time when he arose looking more disheveled than before. Adanta was glad for any pause, for she longed to poke around the town. Most people seemed to be inside, gathered about fires for supper. She caught glimpses of a child with a gravy-soaked piece of corn bread, a big-hipped woman ladling from a pot, a stubble-faced man snoring in a patch of weeds. But the tents were fascination enough, whether furry or smooth or woven, and here and there were windowless cabins and tiny one-room houses made of bent saplings sheathed in bark. All were wildly decorated. Here was a cowhide tent surrounded by a hundred wooden wands—pinwheels, some busily whirring, some still or barely revolving, all made from heavy paper and each fastened to its stick with a shiny nail. Next door stood a woven tent striped mulberry and indigo, hung with pennants and ribbons and looking like a jester's cap. Beyond it, with dozens of tiny moth holes stitched up in coarse green string, was a rose-colored tent limp and soft enough to have been in the family for many generations.

"*There* it is," Magpie Joe reported from his lookout on top of a crate of chickens. His hands made a fluttery motion in the air, and it seemed to Adanta that he lifted a few inches off the box. As she bent to peer at his feet, he jumped down and began thread-ing his way through the maze of tents, eyes on a point unseen. When he abruptly wheeled about, she bumped into him, causing a flurry of protest inside the coat.

His mouth became a straight line, and he glanced at her in annoyance. Again she had the feeling that his feet were not set on anything solid.

"Sorry, sorry," she offered, trying to peep under the hem of his coat.

He croaked a protest, rose another inch, and caught hold of a tent pole.

"Dear me," he said faintly, a surprised look float-ing into his eyes.

Here he snatched at Adanta and called for her to help him to the ground. Soon he was once more headfirst on the earth. This time, very slowly, he pushed himself into an upside-down position. In the initial stage his back was up but his legs were still folded, so that he looked something like a frog; then the coat spilled open, displaying its many gaily sewn pockets and the cap-beaked heads of birds; and fi-nally the thin legs with their knobby knees went up, wavering, cautious, but up. He stayed thus for some minutes, while Adanta walked around and around him, taking a sharp glance at his woven striped trousers and the purple socks, and then looking one by one at the birds.

Curling over, he landed with a thump on the grass.

"Seldom have I been so"—and here he paused, pondering—"so very remarkably light-headed."

Adanta offered him a hand, and slowly he made it back onto his feet.

"You haven't any relatives who are birds, have you?" he asked. "No auntie who hatched out of a shell? No down under your hair at the base of your neck? No old daddy with a bit of wing-sheath poking out of his back? Nothing?"

She shook her head no.

"Pity," he said; "makes one's life so much more interesting, doesn't it?"

"Well," Adanta replied, "I suppose it would, wouldn't it?" This, too, sounded to her ears like something he might say, and she wondered whether he might be beginning to rub off on *her*, the way the birds clearly rubbed off on *him*.

"Curious, though," he mused; "I thought that might explain the extraordinary light-headedness. I could have sworn that my feet were paddling the air. And that hasn't happened to me for a very long time. Not since—the first lyric flights of youth—back when I first met my Caledonia—when she had to tether me with a sky-blue ribbon. Still," he added quietly, "it was an intensely pleasurable experience.

"And maybe you just don't know the minor branches of your family tree," he continued. "I had an ancestor who was a good Scots rook, or so my granfer claimed, and another who was enchanted his whole life and spent half of each year as a swan in Coole Park. They say he loved his swan mate better than his human wife and that all the rest of the year he was homesick for the lime trees and sycamores beside the lake."

Placing a hand on his heart, Magpie Joe began to declaim in a loud voice: "His grief was terrible when the lady swan died; no bird could comfort him, and all the rest of his life there was nothing that made him glad but the lapping of water on stone and the cold streams high in the air." He shrugged, adding, "Or so it's said in the handed-down tales. They're rather poetical. I expect that's the swan in us—what makes our clan so turbulent-hearted and romantic."

"So sad."

"But you see he had it—his great love. You see? When so many do not."

He gently detached a grasshopper from his lapel and set it down on the grass, before speaking again.

"However 'tis with you, I suspect some plumage on your ancestral twigs."

Picking up his crushed hat, he brushed it off and put it back on his head. Just before he tugged it into place, Adanta noticed that his hair was now tumbled about, peppered with crumbs of dirt and bits of straw.

"Onward," he said softly, opening the coat to check on his birds. "I feel the need to rest and nest. I need my Caledonia, my Callie, my sweet Cal."

He teetered off, so unsteady that after a few moments Adanta took his arm and helped him straighten up.

"Dear child," he said, patting her hand, "what a dear thing it is."

She thought of saying, "I'm not an *it*," but held her tongue. Just walking seemed hard enough for him now.

Yet he had no trouble finding the tent. He seemed to have regained his sense of direction, and as he moved surely toward his goal, he began to cheer up and now and then to whoop with anticipation.

"Straight as the crow flies, dear child," he called airily, stepping between a sloppy homespun shelter and another one that resembled a partly molted buffalo.

"Here, indeed, we are," he announced, indicating a tent that she would have had no trouble identifying as his own even if he hadn't guided her there.

Gray-black and glossy, wing-shaped panels hung over a framework of crooked poles. From the peak tumbled dozens of crinkled silvery strips of tin and foil that made a faint shivering noise in the slight breeze.

"Home," he said fondly, pulling aside the door flap.

Nothing, not even Magpie Joe's melodious trilling of her very long name, could have prepared the girl for Caledonia, who sat chin in hand, gazing into the fire. For she was no match to her husband—no spry, birdlike stick figure with knobby knees—but an immense statue of a woman with heavy arms, massive legs, and a strong and handsome profile. Caledonia could not be called fat, although she was huge. Rather, she looked like certain sculptures that seem to rejoice in bold lines and big curves. She appeared to be half-asleep and only slowly roused herself to stare at them as Magpie Joe carefully outspread his coat and fastened it to the walls of the tent, where it hung like a living mural, glistening with eyes. Then he sprang to his wife's side and buried his face against her neck. Stroking his head as if he were a baby, she murmured to him.

"And a child," Adanta heard him say. He sank down at Caledonia's feet and, smiling gleefully, pointed across the tent.

"It's an ill luck to point." Caledonia heaved up a sigh, her glance drifting across the birds.

"Come, birdling," Magpie Joe called, gesturing toward Adanta.

The woman swept a glance over the girl, observing with a whisper that she "needs clothes and looks like a boy in those jeans.

"I don't need a child," Caledonia went on. "I already have my Joe." Magpie Joe was now sitting on the earth at her feet, and she had begun combing the trash from his hair while he whistled to the pet magpie on his finger. Reaching down, she patted his cheek. "He's my sweet boy, my bird man."

"But I don't want to belong to you," Adanta explained. "I'm searching for my parents. I followed your husband to the Pony Fair, hoping to find somebody who might have seen them. Or who could call them home." And she told what had happened to Jess and Charlotte, telling it slowly so that she would forget nothing.

At the end of the story, Caledonia let go of another sigh. It seemed to Adanta that she breathed seldom, perhaps because she was so looming-large—

although that was silly, she supposed, as if a woman were a creature like a whale, which only occasionally came up for air.

"So you're not an outlander, after all. I was afraid my Joe might be getting us into trouble. He does occasionally, selling his birds to people outside Adantis. We have places we go to trade with foreigners, but we don't want them coming inside. There are too many here already, tramping over the mountains for fun—as if walking weren't to get somewhere—and digging up what's left of the Cherokee mothertowns. We don't want the taint, don't want them tearing up what's not meant to be torn. But you're half-Adantan, half-foreign—a borderer, from the edge of Adantis. And we Adantans are all part borderers from the lost world of the northern Britons, so say the History Tellers. We're part borderers and part natives of the place, Cherokee with maybe a splash of some spot else thrown in—a trace of Africa maybe, or a fleck of Daneland and the Viking warriors who used to raid the coasts of the Old World, a smidge of England or Wales—like Colonel Thomas of the Legion.

"About your mother and father . . ." Caledonia paused, rubbing her arms as if she were cold. "I can't call them to come here or anywhere. These things happen, not often, but they happen. Everybody pays attention to the ancient sayings and watches out for a curse or a charm, yet only a few people become wizards. You should go to the witchmaster and to the Teller of Wonders. But get a proper gown so the people don't gawk at you."

The girl nodded, glancing up when the minute droppings of a finch streaked her wrist. She found it hard to grasp all that Magpie Joe's wife said, because Caledonia had such a thick, broad drawl—an accent much stronger than Adanta's—and she wondered whether her own voice might not also sound strange to some of the Hidden People.

During her account, Magpie Joe had begun to release the smaller birds, which whirled about the dome before settling down to sip and to bathe in a bowl of water and to eat from a plate of seed near the fire. Now he was freeing the larger birds, and one by one they flew up to the crooked limbs that crossed the tent just below the roof. When she noticed an immense bird, perhaps a rook, directly over her head, Adanta shifted her seat.

"Well, nobody'll be out and about till later. There's such a rumpus in the day that they're all frazzled by supper. Some of them drink too much moonshine and need a lie-down." Caledonia laughed. "Those big fellows were reared up on whiskey, doled in a baby's cup or sucked from a rag."

"No more," Magpie Joe broke in.

"We can learn a few things from the foreigners, and that's one," she added, "although I can't rightly think of another. Here," she said, raking in the fire with a stick; "you traipsers must be hungry."

"Peckish," the bird man admitted.

The idea that she would have them eat live coals passed through Adanta's mind before she realized that something was cooking in the ashes. It took only a minute for Caledonia to scoop a batch of narrow tubers out of the fire, wipe them off, and drop them into bowls along with some boiled greens. Soon Adanta was chewing on what proved to be tough-skinned small potatoes. They had a nutty taste, not like what she was used to at home.

"They're good," she said in surprise, for she could hardly believe that potatoes would be, without butter or salt.

"Eat up, and then you can go around the fair. People just pour out of the woods in the evening. The children will start shrieking around the alleys, and then the other folks will be out, haggling or hawking goods. Joe and I'll be pinning up the door flap and selling birds." Caledonia gestured at a jumble of cages woven from young tree shoots, some peeled and some with the bark left on. "That's what I do, gather the withies and weave houses for birds. They're nice enough."

Politely, Adanta went over to inspect them and found the cages just as fanciful and alluring as the Pony Fair itself. There were wicker palaces topped with tinsel and crinkled metal; there were small cabins where the birds could sleep; and there were huts which came with a big velvet cap.

Caledonia was pleased with the girl's enthusiasm, looking at her through lowered lashes and smiling.

"You scoot along," she said, "and come back when it's time for bed. You can sleep here—it's the last night of the fair."

When Adanta stepped from the tent, pack slung over her shoulder, she realized that because the Pony Fair was planted so deep in the mountains, it had already gone pitch-dark—probably the fairgrounds had grown dim long before sunset. An old man was shuffling about with a can of kerosene, filling and firing the torches that had been thrust into the ground every ten feet or so. She could hear men calling to one another, the startled neighing of horses, and a wavering music somewhere close by.

The Pony Robbers, she guessed; *but what was the other sound?*

At the end of the alley was a bough-strewn hut and seven or eight children sitting together in the grass outside, barefoot and dressed in homespun. Each held a stringed bow that ranged in size from less than two feet long to what was surely more than five. From these came eerie trembles, one plucked vibration after another. The notes echoed in the children's mouths—for an end of each bow rested between a child's open lips. Her hand lighting on a coarsely woven tent, Adanta watched them play. A breeze came up, and she could not tell whether it was the cool air or the music that gave her such a strange, shivery sensation. Behind her the sounds of the Pony Fair grew louder, but the noise could not drown out the uncanny humming. The moon drifted up from the mountaintop, snagged in a great balsam, and then floated free. She found herself wishing that she, too, could live in Adantis—that somewhere in the fair there would be a tent hung all around with carved bears and raccoons and deer and birds, that inside she would find Ba, teaching some child how to read or else to multiply and divide the world of things, and Mama, sitting on a throne of peeled wood with the beautiful litter of shavings in pale heaps around her feet. Closing her eyes, she wished hard, her longing flying up in a prayer that quivered with the strings, that she knew could touch the moon and soar farther than the stars—when abruptly she was knocked down onto the grassy path.

"Watch where you're loitering," growled a voice.

Blinking, Adanta opened her eyes, seeing first a wobbling image of the children on the firelit green grass with song-bows in their mouths, before catching view of a high black outline. As he stepped into the light, Adanta's mouth slipped open: she was looking at the biggest man she had ever seen, a red-haired fellow squinting against the firelight and rubbing his head.

"What an ache," he groaned. Catching sight of her again, he glared and spat tobacco juice into a big bowl outside a potter's tent.

"You're a *Messer*," Adanta exclaimed, suddenly realizing that this enormous, redheaded fellow with the bloodshot eyes and tangled hair must be one of her own neighbors.

The huge man ripped out a yell, and the children jumped to their feet, picking up the song-bows. When he made a fist in exasperation, they scuttled into the leafy hut, the youngest one bawling for his mother.

"My name is Taliaferro Messer," the giant bellowed, "and you're nothing but a foreigner's brat!"

Waves of sweet-stinking whiskey breath washed over Adanta, who stepped backward and scampered down the alley, her pack bumping against her as she fled. She tripped, picked herself up, and shot onward, past a peddler carrying a smoked rack of frogs-on-a-stick, past a ribbon hawker with love knots bunched all over her dress, past children gathered around a storyteller. Darting swiftly around tents and sacks and boxes, she at last saw in front of her the blessed gloom outside the Pony Fair—and then it was, speeding full-tilt toward the night, that she slammed smack into someone else: the other emitted a piercing cry of surprise and tumbled forward, toppling her in the fall.

"Excuse me," came a vaguely familiar male voice.

"Sorry—my fault, really," she replied, winded. "Shouldn't—shouldn't have been running—not on the path—not in the dark."

A hand gripped hers, pulling her into the torch-light. The girl kept her face down, embarrassed.

"Thought it was somebody I knew," a triumphant voice said as Adanta looked up and saw that there, his face older and thinner and streaked with tears, was the Pony Boy.

Tassel and the Fair of Wonders

After Adanta had poured out the whole long story of how she had lost her father and mother and set out to search for them, the Pony Boy gave a low whistle. For several minutes the two lay silently in the grass, she leaning on one arm with her eyes on the lit tents of the fair and he with his hands laced behind his head, staring up at the clear night sky and its dazzle of stars.

"I liked your mother," he said, when he spoke at last.

"You did? After she sent you away like that?"

"Well, she was right, wasn't she? Who was I? Some boy from the west, from unknown regions. She must've sensed it could be dangerous. Foreign places always are, because you don't know how they work. My mother hates it when I leave Adantis on one of my adventures."

He plucked a long stem of grass and began tearing it to bits, staining his nails.

"All the same, I do," he added. "I've been in the Lands Beyond past Cullowhee, to Caney Fork, just to see the Judaculla Rock with the pictographs. Then once I was out for weeks, and I got lost and thought I'd never get home again. Because it's so celebrated in our tales, I rode all the way to the old Nikwasi Mound in Franklin, but I didn't like it much. It was all hemmed in by the town, and you could see that the Nunnehi would hate it that way."

Adanta nodded, though unsure what he meant. She too had seen the Judaculla Rock, with cows cropping the grass on either side. As for Franklin, she remembered gem shops with crystals and geodes on the doorsteps and a big mound with a state marker close by. Was it famous?

"I couldn't feel them anywhere around, and all I could think was that the Nunnehi had left that place forever," he continued.

"What are they?"

"Nunnehi? Don't you know? I thought everyone would know, even outlanders. They are Cherokee spirit people who love the balds and peaks and live in invisible townhouses. And they're not seen, either, unless they choose to show themselves. They're well known for helping people who are lost, and I still think that I've met one of the Nunnehi—when I was wandering in the forest, he fed me and gave me a map. He knew about Adantis, because he drew a ragged shape on the map that my father later said was the original boundary line. But I don't know for sure. That was the time I went to see the Nikwasi Mound, where the soldiers from the United States turned back because they thought they saw many handsome, straight warriors guarding the town, but really it was the Nunnehi. That was in the Civil War. Haven't you heard that story? Or the one about Wilusdi and the Thomas Legion of Cherokee who fought for the Confederate States?"

Adanta stared at him.

"Terrible not to know your own history. That's partly an outlander story, but our History Tellers know about it. They tell about the battles and about the death of Astugataga, back in the Civil War. About how the Cherokee in the end fought on both sides and almost destroyed one another."

"Astugataga—it's the Lean One's name," Adanta cried out. "But you say he's dead."

"That was long ago. And not an uncommon name,

Astugataga being a hero in the mountains." The Pony Boy shrugged, rolling over on his side to inspect her.

"You look about the same as before," he said. "Taller."

"You look different," she told him. "Older. Your face is—how old are you?"

Again he shrugged. "What does it matter? My mother might be able to figure it out."

"You don't know? Don't know how old you are?" Adanta sat up, staring at him.

"I know I'm old enough to perch on Looking-Glass Rock. Old enough to help with trading outside Adantis. And I've been old enough to go to the Lands Beyond by myself for three summers now," he said stoutly. "That's what being grown is about."

"Well," Adanta said, "then I guess I'm getting older by the second, because everything I do lately is something I've never done before."

Pulling out her grandmother's stole, she wrapped herself in its warmth. The ground was cooling moment by moment as the stars grew brighter and the sky turned a deeper blue.

"You never told me your name," she said softly, wondering whether he cared about a name if he didn't care about his age.

"One of my grandmothers calls me *Agili*, or 'He-is-rising.' The other one calls me Thomas, because we are related to the Welshman Thomas. He was adopted as son by the Cherokee chief Drowning-Bear, and he became a great chief of the tribe, like his father before him. It was a long time ago, but we still remember it. Most everybody else just calls me Tassel, after Utsidsata—Old Tassel. Or else just Tass."

He looked at her, then added, "He was chief during the Revolutionary War. That's part of your history and Adantan history, too. You know about the war?"

"Of course I do." Somehow the Pony Boy made her feel ignorant, even though she was the one who had gone to school and studied with Ba.

He must have sensed that Adanta was a little offended, because he didn't say anything for a long time, closing his eyes and lying perfectly still in the grass. He looked changed from what she remembered—several inches taller, and the straight dark hair hung halfway down his back. Although the skin was still olive, his features seemed bolder than she remembered, the forehead and cheekbones high, the upper lip curled almost scornfully, the line of the jaw bold and firm. He was dressed a little differently, too, with leather gaiters almost to the knee over brown homespun pants. The shirt was home-woven as well, open at the neck and cinched with a belt at the waist.

"Tass, Tassel," she whispered, getting used to the name.

When he opened his eyes, she again noticed the dried streak of salt on one cheek.

"What was the matter? Something happened to you, didn't it?" Adanta leaned over him, inspecting the gray eyes.

"Nothing like losing a mother and father." Tassel's gaze lingered on the stole. "That's Adantan, that weaving, isn't it? Your grandmother? In the corn maze?"

She nodded, waiting for him to tell.

"It's Polk." Tassel rubbed a hand through his hair, yanking on a lock as if to distract himself from the words. "He was young enough that they wanted him. Everybody knows him because we go all over Adantis together—it could've been anybody."

"They *who?*"

He continued talking as though he hadn't heard, still tugging at his hair. "It was just yesterday; I was sleeping out in the open." As he told the story and Adanta listened, she was caught up by the tale, picturing him lying in the sun, his hair thrown back and his arms flung out as if he had been wrestled and thrown by sleep. The pony wandered along the edge of a brook, cropping grass and flowers, halting to drink the fast-running water that tumbled down from the high crags, spilling rubies and sapphires onto the valley floor. Farther, farther the horse grazed, following the splashing and singing creek as the first shadows of dusk crept from the mountain-sides, sliding down the gorge. With the darkness came the horse thieves, down from their strongholds in the high ground. The pony lifted his head once, twice, sniffing the air as Tass woke, alerted by a thread of tension, no more substantial than a spider's frail line of web. He started up, spinning about to check the sun, the crest of the mountains, the clumps of balsam, and in turning caught a quivering motion in the distant trees. He was uneasy, gazing down the valley. *The horse was too far.* Shouting *Polk, Polk, Polk,* he waved his arms, but the pony's head was low to the water and the thunder of rapids blotted out the cries. On his arms the hair prickled. Alarm mounted up, sending him charging along the banks, but even as he ran, he saw the laughing pony robbers pour out of the trees. Polk raised his head and stepped a single step back before they flowed around him in a hooting, jostling mass of men and horses. They must have tied a lead rein to him—to Polk, who had never known a harness of any kind! The sun wheeled behind the crags, leaving behind only a few of its glittering spokes. Shadows piled on Tass, but he could see the thieves, milling about in a shaft of light. With a high-pitched yell the robbers spurred their mounts and stampeded down the valley, kicking up dust clouds and stones. Cackling, making the calls of turkeys and owls and crows, the band galloped directly toward him, their jeers swelling louder. Polk screamed with fright, and for an instant Tass saw the mustang leap, his mane waving in the air, the whites of his eyes showing, before he was jerked downward into the clamor of pounding hooves. Then the noise of clumping and neighing and catcalls surrounded Tass like an animal river, and he was knocked from one mare or stallion to another and dashed to the ground, rolling over on his face and praying not to be trampled, not to be kicked.

The flood of horseflesh streamed on; the rumble lessened; and after a time he could hear nothing but cicadas and katydids, like an infinite number of songbows playing to the night and the pony robbers and the pulse of Tassel's grief. Their shimmering curtain of music drowned all other noises except the one of

Tass hollering *Polk, Polk, Polk* in the wilderness. And the sound seemed all the more grief-stricken because it was a young man's voice that broke in places as he cried out against the dark and the great loneliness of the mountains that he had never known before.

Adanta closed her eyes, feeling the far-off valley like an immense well of sorrow.

"That was sad, sadder than anything."

"No," Tass said, "not sadder than anything. There are a thousand things sadder."

Glancing at the Pony Boy, Adanta again felt that she appeared childish and ignorant. She didn't like it, and she thought he knew because he touched her arm and smiled.

"All the same, I'm glad that you took it that way. As sadder than anything. That's good. Because I mean to be a Teller like my father, though I don't know what I'll tell, whether history or the sacred stories or children's tales or something else."

He stood up, brushing a confetti of torn grass from his trousers.

"Look," he said abruptly, "you need some different clothes if you're going to be Adantan. You can't go anywhere without the people noticing you if you're dressed like a boy. Girls don't dress like boys in Adantis."

"That's what Caledonia said, to get a dress."

"You don't have any money, do you? Adantan money?"

"No," she began, then corrected herself: "Well, yes, I do." She dug in the pack for the coins bound up in a rag, unknotting it and dumping them out in the grass. Tass kneeled down, picking through them one by one.

"It's lucky for you that my mother raised me right. This is quite a bit of gold," Tass cautioned, "so don't let anybody else know, not even Magpie Joe and Caledonia. No reason to tempt people. That's what my mother always says. There are good and bad in Adantis, just as in the Lands Beyond. One of these will buy clothes and food enough for a journey. Better tie up the rest of it and make sure it's safe."

He hesitated, considering, his eyes on Adanta.

"Where are you going next?"

"I don't know for certain, but somebody called Cucumber told Magpie Joe that an old lady with my grandmother's name lived seven or eight miles west of here. That she had a mean husband—and I believe that's right. So I thought maybe I would go that way."

"This is what I'm thinking; I'll help you get what you need at the fair, and I'll go with you as far as the

Messers' summer place. The fellows who stampeded me, they looked tall as giants. I'm thinking it was those Messer boys on their big horses that took my Polk. He's not here. I've looked through all the corrals, even the ones that they hide in the woods because people might spot their own horses. The Messer place is due west about four miles, right close to our cabin."

Smiling, Adanta nodded. He was still her old Pony Boy, who would give her a ride if he could.

She was glad he was there; it was more fun to go around the fair with Tass, who swiftly steered her by the hulking men who belched and grunted as she passed.

"Fair trash," he whispered. "Moonshine really draws them out of their dens."

The first stop they made was for clothes, not because he thought them the most pressing thing but because he knew a certain weaver to be fair with money; Adanta needed honest change for her gold coin. He refused to help her pick out a gown, even when she confessed that she had no idea what to do, and said he would wait outside. When she begged, he ducked under the door flap to "make sure you're not cheated," then hunched in a corner scowling at Mrs. Terrell while she brought out gown after gown.

It was nothing like buying a dress with Mama. These were packed up in trunks with bunches of lavender, and there was only one mirror, in which a buyer might see a flash of waist or hem but little more. Mrs. Terrell was a big grandmotherly woman, wearing a dress of her own homespun and a leaf-green cap over her hair. Round and dressed in deep red, with pins stuck over her bosom, she looked to Adanta like a pincushion in the shape of a tomato. Mrs. Terrell clicked her tongue and chided Adanta for the mud-streaked jeans, insisting that she wash her hair and bathe in a tin tub before putting on new clothes. At this, Tass drifted back out the door and did not return. While she was letting Mrs. Terrell pour lukewarm water over her head, several shoppers came in and inspected some caps without a glance at the tub. *They don't care. A naked person in the middle—well, practically—of the room is nothing to them,* Adanta thought, ducking her head and feeling more a stranger than ever. "I need a screen," she told the weaver, who rolled her eyes, then laughed and pinned up a length of cloth when the girl complained that she was blushing all the way to her toes. When she stood up, her own body looked unfamiliar, more muscular than she'd ever seen it. Hunger had narrowed her waist.

The hair was tangled on her shoulders, so Mrs. Terrell made her buy a comb and then proceeded to rake out the knots. "Witches," she hissed, crossing her fingers, "you've had the wild woods witches dancing reels in your hair." Adanta gave her a sideways glance and didn't reply.

Glad to be out of the hard tub, which she was sure had stamped a pattern of concentric rings on her backside, Adanta pulled on a long-sleeved undershift to try on clothes. Mrs. Terrell rooted through her chests, mumbling "Plenty of room to walk, plenty of room to walk." With a triumphant "This!" she pulled out a mulberry-colored woven gown, quite full, with a cinched waist. She dropped it over the girl's head, adding a green braided belt. "That's a pretty thing," the weaver said, admiring her handiwork. Adanta searched in her pack for the last of her clean socks and underwear, deciding that she could go only so far in her change of dress. She would keep her leather hiking boots, which had been specially made for her slim feet and were sturdy and plain, with high lacings. They didn't look out of place under the dress. Then, picking up her stole, she folded the cloth into a triangle and tied it around her shoulders.

"I know that work!" Mrs. Terrell fingered the shawl.

"Birdie Ann. We were of an age—just the same. I'd know it in the deepest sleep. Nobody else in Adantis makes a ring stole, and nobody else could make one like this. It could fly through a baby's pinkie ring—so soft and warm and fine. She's a wonder."

"My grandmother," Adanta told her.

"You be careful how you pick your grandmothers," the weaver said, crossing her fingers again. "Or your grandfathers, that is. Birdie Ann's man is dangerous. She never chose him, but she had to bide with his pick. That's what people said after he snatched her away."

"Do you know where she lives?"

Mrs. Terrell shook her head. "Not for sure, but a year ago I did some bartering with a peddler, and I recognized a piece of cloth in his pack as Birdie Ann's work. The colors, the fineness of the weaving, the pattern—it just spoke to me. Where did he get it? I asked him. He said he'd gotten lost up on the ridges, had been attacked by a big bird. Sure enough, there was a fresh scar around one eye. He had found help up there on the mountaintops. An old woman had tended to the wound. When he was bandaged and fed, she did some trading with him and sent him on his way."

"How can I get there?"

"It's west of here, maybe nine miles, maybe less. When you come to a place where there's a lone graveyard, with shells from the ocean on the mounds to catch the ghosts, then you're nigh the path. But what mountaintop it is, I can't remember. The path, though, he said it was mazy—as corkscrewed as one of your tangles. You'll know by the hairpin curves."

"You were just the same age," the girl said slowly. "But my grandmother looks so old, much older than you."

The other woman clucked her tongue, tears coming to her eyes.

"It's a shame what living with a terrible man can do. Fierce, with a stare that could drain the spunk right out of you. That's what her brother told me, years back. They never got over losing her that way, and people said it killed her mother. We were playmates once, me and Birdie Ann. I'm glad to see her granddaughter and to fit her out right. What else can I do for you?"

After choosing an extra undershift, Adanta pronounced herself "done." Pushing aside the door flap, she called to Tass, who was talking to the children with the song-bows, each of the musicians now busily consuming the legs from roasted frogs-on-a-stick. He drifted over, stopping to examine her, his eyes traveling from the boots peeping out below her skirts to the freshly washed, wavy hair. Very slowly a smile dawned on his face.

"That's more like it," he said, although adding a little doubtfully, "but I still think you'll get noticed."

With Tass's help, Adanta paid, receiving a shower of silver in exchange. "Caledonia said to see a witch-master and the Teller of Wonders," she whispered as they left the shop.

He let out a groan. "I don't like any of the witch-masters, but I suppose you must."

It was lovely to blend in with the Adantans. Tass grasped her hand, and she let him guide her along the grass paths while she stared at the people in the torchlight and at the pennants and odd peaks and domes of the Pony Fair. Adanta noticed that he was always alert to the sounds of horses, watching who was arriving, who departing. The witchmasters' row of huts lay at the back of the tent town. After some dithering over what Tass said were the two best choices, a crookbacked little woman named Maude Ross or a Messer, he chose the Messer because, after all, *he* wanted to know more about the Messers and their doings.

A glossy holly tree grew by the door, catching at Adanta's ring stole.

Drawing aside the curtain, she stepped inside, her hand still in Tass's. She tightened her grip on him, seeing nothing but a dim fire and wisps passing up and out of the smoke hole. A shuffling noise made her press close, and the boy reminded her that they would need silver.

"What was it you called the Messers, back when we rode through the corn maze?" she whispered.

"Sssh. It must have been *Tsunil kalu*. A long time ago, before there was an Adantis, back in the seventeenth century, a party of giants came out of the West and met with the Cherokee. They must have stayed a year or more, and when they left to go back home, it's said that three of them would not go because they wanted to marry Cherokee women. When the settlers invaded what is now Adantis, the descendants of the giants moved deep into the mountains. Some of the History Tellers say they were the first Hidden People. Later on, a group of settlers intermarried with them, and there are several clans of giants in the deep coves. No one bothers them because they're pretty stout fighters, and—"

A flame appeared in the darkness, moving from the rear of the hut. Its light seemed far away, although from the outside the witchmaster's booth had appeared quite small. As the candle came closer,

Adanta saw that it was held by a huge gnarled hand. Closer still, and she could see the great hooded face with its grizzled beard and drooping pocked nose. The Messer giant's head brushed the ceiling; when he lowered himself onto a stump fixed in the ground, the hut trembled.

Swiftly Tass stepped forward and presented a coin to the witchmaster.

The old man pocketed it without a glance and looked keenly at Adanta.

"You already have protection, I see," he said, nodding at the amulet around her neck. Instinctively she put her hand up and felt the little bag. "What do you want from me?"

She told him about her father's search for the healing lake, about the Lean One and the blue window frames, about how her mother sleepwalked away and vanished, about the grandmother and her cruel husband.

"There is a mystery here," the witchmaster muttered. "I can do little to shelter you from it beyond what your grandmother has given you. But you must not dabble in charms or home-brewed potions. Do not be tempted to attack the wizard with sacred formulas or by witchcraft. It is possible to destroy a sorcerer by carving the image of his heart into a holly tree and driving a spike into that heart for nine days. There are other ways, long and risky. You must not follow such a path. You must remain as clear and pure as the healing lake itself, and then the Spirit who guides our walks and days will protect you. You know, do you, what Mooney says about the Raven Mocker?"

"She is unlearned," Tass told him.

"Perhaps that is for the best," the witchmaster said in a voice so low they could barely make out his words. "In Adantis, innocence is itself a charm against sorcery. I do not know if the Lean One whom you name is a Raven Mocker. When you see him, if your heart tells you it is so, then speak out and name him. Naming is all it takes to slay his power. Once he is recognized, all his life and strength dribble away in seven days. Do not say the words unless you are sure, or you may cause some other harm. Yet you must not be afraid to speak, though he dies."

"I cannot *kill* him," Adanta protested.

"Then your mother may be destroyed if the man is indeed a Raven Mocker. Or she may become ruined like him, a feeder on the lives of others. And you must remember that you do not kill. You only *see* what he is and say it. That is all. What evil does to him is the result of his own choosing and was decided long ago."

There was a long silence, in which the enormous witchmaster sighed, his lips making a loud *f-f-f-f-i-i-i-p-p* sound.

"Be pure," he repeated.

"And what about my friend, whose pony has been stolen? What can be done for him?"

"I can speak for myself, and for my horse," Tass began, but the other two ignored him.

The witchmaster reached out his leathery hand, and Adanta hurriedly placed another of the silver coins upon it. He leaned back, his eyes twinkling.

"And has it been done by witchcraft?"

"Hah! Not likely," Tass exclaimed.

"I think perhaps it has been done by Messercraft," Adanta said boldly.

The witchmaster looked stern, then began trembling, then hooted out loud. He roared, so that they could see his greenish teeth and the roof of his mouth, looking as big and uneven as the underside of a turtle's shell.

"You're a funny, valiant maid." He wiped the tears from his cheeks with a sleeve. "Did I not tell you that innocence is a charm? Here's the proof of it, for

I will help you against my own kind. My prediction is that the boy may indeed get his pony back, but in the process he may lose something he values even more unless he is careful. However, he cannot be in two places at once, so he had better not worry about it. Also, observation tells me that caves make mighty fine places in which to hide horses, especially small ones. That's just personal, mind you, some family experience—not the advice of a witchmaster."

Thanking him, Adanta groped in her pocket for a third piece of silver and offered it to the old man.

"Good luck to you, little one," he called out, snuffing his candle and leaving them to feel for a passage out of the hut.

In the alley, Tass thanked Adanta, rather stiffly, for spending her money on him. Lost in her memory of the giant witchmaster, Adanta did not answer as she followed him down the winding paths. When the boy slowed, searching for the Teller of Wonders, she at last spoke. "He probably calls anybody who's not a Messer a *little one.*"

After pacing the length of the Tellers' alley, which was at this hour almost deserted—the younger children having already fallen asleep after a day playing in the fresh mountain air, the women at work or tending the sleepers, the men carousing in the moonshine alley—Tass looked puzzled and said he could not find the Teller of Wonders. There was a History Teller, a white-haired old man, in his windowless Cherokee cabin, with a tattered regimental flag on a staff stuck into the ground before the door. There was a young woman, a Teller of Animal Stories, curled up to sleep on a pile of skins in her lodge, which resembled a beaver's mound of sticks and logs. And there was a site devoted to a Teller of Sacred Stories, with a feathered and beaded cross mounted above his closed tent flap.

"I don't know." Tass paused, then took Adanta's hand and led the way into the darkness beyond the last stall. "Always, always, there's at least one Teller of Wonders. You can't have the Pony Fair without one. Last year it was Jeb Shook. He has a maypole outside his lodge, a bay staff all tied up in ribbons. Maybe he left early. Maybe I missed him."

In the deep shadow of the mountains, they could make out a thin radiance and minute specks that flashed and shone.

"What is it?" Adanta let go Tass's hand and sped forward, halting as she saw a glimmering on each side of a grassy path—phosphorescent mushrooms and the pale, glowing stems of Indian pipes. At the end of the walkway was a tent, half-transparent and as delicately woven as the grandmother's ring stole. From the peak fluttered a length of—what? not cloth surely, though woven it must be—something as fine-spun as a mountaintop cloud and shining with evanescent colors. Half-hidden by the fabric, fireflies rose from the ground, their lights flaring and dying away, and a small form gleamed as palely as the Indian pipes. Now and then six or seven fireflies shot out the smoke hole and rose up to mingle with the stars.

"Wait," Tass called, but Adanta's fingers were already on the door.

"Come in." The silvery voice was like a chime, so lovely that she couldn't help pulling aside the veil and entering.

Dazzled, Adanta could make out nothing but the glittering threads of the tent and the streaking flight paths of the fireflies. She closed her eyes, stepped foward, and opened them again. Standing on a chunk of sapphire was a figure hardly taller than a six-year-old child. Adanta breathed shallowly, feeling the air to be chill and mountain-sharp. Behind her Tass ducked to come in, and she could hear his intake of breath. The spirit being laughed, again with the silvery sound of bells.

"I am Lalu, and I will tell you a tale of Wonder."

The girl shook back the pale waterfall of hair that poured down past her feet—a flood almost white, had it not glowed faintly with the moonbow's colors. "And someday you, Adanta, will pay me back with bone of your bone. It is already foretold and written in our secret histories. *Ku!* Hear me.

"Once there was an outlander girl who was searching for the Gall Place, because she was sick to death. She climbed over many mountain ranges, but she could not find the healing lake. At last she became lost and wandered for many weeks until she chanced upon one of the Yunwi Tsunsdi, who showed her that, indeed, she already stood on its shores. No sooner had the Yunwi Tsunsdi said the word than the waves, the color of sapphire, began to lap out of the rocks, and the girl felt a thrill as the water climbed her legs. A hound-bitten stag, a rabbit torn by a fox, a bear with wounded paw crept into the water. The stag bounded away, the rabbit hopped and frisked for joy, and the bear lumbered up the shore and began raking blueberries from the brush. Eager to embrace its healing, the girl dived into the lake and disappeared. So long had she dreamed of swimming its depths, so beautiful was her longing, that she was transformed into a trout, the rainbow painted along her side, and even after the lake ebbed and sank into

126

the earth, she played and leaped in the mountain streams."

Adanta listened, and she felt afraid for her father—what did it mean? And how could she pay with "bone of her bone"? Did the creature want her very life? The histories, the foretelling: all was mist and mystery.

"Please, tell us more." Tass drew close to the Teller of Wonders, but she only laughed.

The silvery noise made Adanta feel light-headed, and she raised a hand to the amulet. Fireflies streaked from the grass, thicker and thicker until she could hardly see Lalu or the walls of the tent; then everything was part of the glistening, and she could only grope for Tass's arm and, dizzier than ever, trip and tumble to the grass. The blaze thinned, fell apart into golden threads like the warp of a loom. One by one, the fireflies flew up like sparks and were lost among the stars. Adanta and Tass knelt on the damp ground, the phosphorescent mushrooms and Indian pipes dimming around them.

Lalu had vanished.

"That was a thing I will never forget," Tass whispered. "I am sure she was a Yunwi Tsunsdi, one of the Little People, and a sight hardly one in a thousand Adantans has ever seen."

To Mossy Creek

"Dear child," Magpie Joe protested, taking out a large spotted handkerchief and wiping a kiss from his cheek.

It seemed to have had a lightening effect on him, for he promptly bent down and tapped his forehead three times on the trampled earth.

"Morning, Tassel," he said calmly, as if there were nothing at all unusual about pressing one's head to the nearest piece of clay.

Tass came up, nodded to Adanta, and shook Magpie Joe's hand, then bent to enter the tent, where Caledonia was boiling squash and corn mush over the fire. A flood of laughter followed his entrance.

" 'Tis a funny child, Tass." Magpie Joe rubbed his brow. "Quite unusual. Well, it's the different ones that turn out to be storytellers, isn't it? His father was an odd chick before him. But Roy's a grand singer and instrument maker and Teller. There's nothing greater than a good Teller. He's a tent spar of Adantis, he is. A great tall mast of a pine in the forest, holding up the Adantan sky."

The girl surveyed the Pony Fair. All was morning bustle, with the taking down of tents and the clatter of pole on pole. Up on the mountainside the children from the brush hut were playing their song-bows again, making a hum that set the deep dell tingling. Tass had said they were second cousins of his, part of the Dills clan, that he would bide with them for the night. Here and there a horse dragged away a stall, its tent and wares bundled together in a makeshift travois. The Messer witchmaster plodded up the grass alley, his storehouse of goods lashed together with strong ropes and fastened to his back. Adanta watched as he expelled a squirt of tobacco like a brown comet. Meeting her eye, the old man let out a shout and fell to choking on his quid. He slapped his chest thunderously and strode out of the encampment. His head was visible for a while before being lost in trees. Along with several other men, another Messer lay flopped in the mud where the moonshine tents had stood. They looked like so many snoring logs.

Fair trash, she remembered.

Yawning, Magpie Joe looked around at the scene, the scampering children in shifts and shirttails, the sweating men and women taking down their Pony Fair homes, the packhorses with their heads down to the grass.

"You sold a lot of birds," Adanta ventured, "a lot of cages."

"Oh, it's terribly sad, isn't it? To lose so many friends? I had to go back home twice during the week just to fetch more." Then he brightened. "But a man's got to live, got to have nest and keep just the same as a bird."

Inside the tent Caledonia was yelling for them to come and eat, and Adanta hurried after her bowl of mush. The corn was hot and blotted out the emptiness in her stomach. And whether or not the mountain air added a sharpness to hunger and a tang to food, she downed the contents of her bowl so quickly that she was back for more even before Tass.

Overhead there were only a few unsold birds, looking forlorn on the big perches. Joe's pet magpie flew down to his shoulder, pecking at his collar until his master began gently scratching the bird's head.

"Poor Scoggins, poor poor poor Scoggins," the magpie croaked; at least, that was how Magpie Joe interpreted his sounds. It was all the bird ever had to say, and why *poor* Scoggins, no one knew.

"Come on," Caledonia called to Tass, "help me take down the supports, now that I've fed you and the girl."

Magpie Joe hurriedly collected his birds, tying on yarn leashes and fastening an end of each to his cap. Adanta carried the remaining cages and cooking pots outside. She wished she could do more to thank the pair for the meals and the use of their tent, but she felt sure they would be offended if she offered to pay. Hadn't Caledonia helped her with advice? And without Magpie Joe she might never have found Tass or met a witchmaster or one of the Little People—she might have marched on through the wilderness in her foreigner's jeans, the Adantans hiding as she passed them, near enough to touch. Only one so addle-headed and gentle as the bird man would have paused to let her attach herself to him—to let her ride his coattails to the fair like a burr or a prickly green nit of beggar-lice.

"Here," Caledonia called from the tent flap, waving a small cage at her, "take it." When she went to put it with the others, the big woman bellowed, "Not there. Hang it from your rucksack, girl."

"For me?"

Magpie Joe beamed. "Because you're a very good sort of child—a very pleasant guest—if we were going to have a fledgling of our own (which we are not, evidently), then we would be happy to have *your* sort of chick, you see. So take it as a token of our admiration."

At this, Adanta hugged him around the neck, which forced him to remove his hat with its attendant birds and repeat his three taps-on-the-head once again.

"It's just a nub of a bird—so, so tiny—what on earth is it?" she asked, lifting up the cage to examine the stumpy-tailed resident.

"*Troglodytes troglodytes,* dear child," Magpie Joe intoned, "also known as the winter wren. Four inches only from tail's tip to top of the head, a round, brown, mouselike, scuttling, head-bobbing birdlet. Tail snubbed off, briefer than on all other native wrens. Lives in Adantis all the year round, and can be told apart from the house wren by the light brow line over the eye and the dark barred underbelly. Slightly downcurved bill. Very lively, scurrying, spry wee chick. Frequents the scrub and conifer woods in her natural setting. Don't let her go; the left wing's not right, didn't set properly at all, but she's a cheerful, happy creature. Sings out with many tinkling warbles and airy trills, high-pitched, often closing with a rather piercing trill. Also a *kep-kep, kep-kep* cry as well. We call her Trog."

"I'll give her another name," Adanta announced. "After all, everything in Adantis seems to have three or four."

She squatted down to examine the wren and the domed cage, which was cleverly made of bent willow shoots and honeysuckle vines and resembled the skeleton of Joe and Caledonia's tent—which was now standing naked without its covering of cloth. Trog sprang from perch to perch, bobbing her head as Magpie Joe had promised. When Adanta put her finger through the vines, the creature hopped upward, the small, briery feet fastening onto her skin.

"I'll call you White Brow," she told the bird, which jumped down and began turning over the litter of fresh leaves and bark on the floor of her cage.

"What does she eat?"

"Spiders, mostly," Magpie Joe said cheerfully. "You can try any insect, although some of them are as big as she is, just about."

"Uh-huh." Adanta felt somewhat dubious about spiders—and about her ability to catch enough of them to fuel the busy little wren.

"Oh, you can let her out where there are no snakes

or owls around—she can find her own food and can't fly far. Just hops, mostly. She can hunt for spiders pretty well, given a choice spot."

Magpie Joe helped her hook the cage onto the side of the grandmother's pack. By that time the frame and perches were down from the tent, and Tass was helping Caledonia load a burro with the couple's belongings.

"I'll miss you both," Adanta whispered.

"Dear child," Joe uttered mournfully, slowly pulling out his handkerchief and giving a loud honk to his nose. A gray down-feather stuck to the tip, making Tass and Adanta laugh. Magpie Joe offered a weak smile, reaching up to remove the feather and let it sail away.

"Goodbye, then." Caledonia clapped her hands together. "Buck up, Joe. It may or may not be forever, and besides, I hate a sour face. We see Tass often enough. And you'll meet the girl again, surely. If not, well then, what can you do about it? No use to fret."

She gave each of them a vigorous hug, ignoring Adanta's attempt at thanks. Smacking the burro on its rump, she marched away, turning once to wave and call to Magpie Joe, who wouldn't depart until Tass and Adanta set off to the west. They paused many times to wave at the dejected figure, stopping at the last possible moment to watch as he tapped his head against the ground three times, rose, set his hat carefully on his head, and flapped his arms in answer to his wife's shout.

"I thought he didn't like me at first." Adanta cast another look over her shoulder, but she could see nothing except green leaves.

"You're all right." Tass grinned, taking her hand and swinging it back and forth.

That was Adantan, too, she reflected. At the fair she had noticed that the children and grownups commonly held hands, pushed and shoved one another, slapped a friend on the shoulder as they passed. Adantans just clung to one another more than people in the Lands Beyond, it seemed.

Kep-kep, kep-kep, kep-kep. White Brow chirped at her back, the cage swinging.

"It'll be rough going soon," Tass told her; "there's a pass, but it's straight up to the top to get there, with a lot of loose shillets underfoot. It'll save us three or four hours this way."

"I don't care," she cried, leaping onto a boulder and down again. "I could walk to the ends of the earth and back." Truly, she felt it was so: that the up-and-down walk to the Pony Fair had hardened her muscles; and far from draining her desire to go on, it had given her fresh energy. She would keep hunting Ba and Mama—would clamber over every mountain in Adantis until she found them.

Despite the rugged ground, steep with poor footing on broken shale, the way to Tassel's house seemed easy and brief compared to the days of struggle that had come before. The reason partly was that it was shorter, the route known, and partly that Caledonia had packed cold wedges of fried grits and several bottles of cider in a sack for Tass to carry. Company was sweet; with somebody to talk to, Adanta never once considered the dangers she had feared, alone—what lurked in the black shadows under heaps of boulders or what would happen if she slid on a crag and was injured. The pair often stopped to let the wind dry the sweat from their faces and to watch the hawks wheel high above.

It was late afternoon when Tass pointed to a spot in the valley and said, "There it is." To Adanta the point was perfectly imaginary, invisible—just one more ivy stitch in a tapestry woven from every shade of green. She couldn't fathom how the boy kept to the path, for what he called a trail was far less visible than the worn lines made by deer in the woods near home. Slowly they wound along the mountainside, pausing once at a rockslide for Tass to pick a bouquet

of flowers and toss it down the precipitous drop—
Adanta leaned over, the wind flinging her hair back,
to see the small white cross and weathered conch
shell that marked the site where nine years back the
boy's oldest brother, Rob, had tumbled to his death.
Fear spread along her spine, like a line of flame
whipped by the breeze. It seemed that the mountains
wanted her to slip on the wobbling siltstone—to see
her fail and fall!

"Come on," Tass said, latching a hand on her wrist
and jerking her away; "it's not a place to stop."

Adanta told herself that she was wrong—there was
nothing the mountains wanted, and if she could
speak for them, she would say only that they wanted
to be, to go on becoming more and more themselves,
with the ravens and hawks riding their high breeze-
ways and the pebbles and streams spilling along their
flanks.

Halfway down the mountainside, Tass let the slope
pull him and began to whoop and race, crashing
through fernbrake and mayapple leaves like a pur-
sued deer. She followed him, pitching forward, the
pack bouncing on her back and White Brow trilling
in pleasure or protest, she did not know which. Her
voice flew out of her mouth like a banner on the
wind, nonsense syllables calling and echoing across

the valley as she jounced downward, jumping the rivulets of icy water, stepping once on a narrow yellow-and-black snake and suddenly going cold to the bone, then thrusting off faster—remembering the sight of a snake handler in a tent at the Pony Fair, his eyes on the big rattler in his grip, hanging stiff and straight like the staff of Moses. Yelling, the boy and girl stumbled through a glade of ferns at the bottom, unable to halt, wild to be running forever.

At last her legs slowed, trembling, and Adanta dropped onto her knees. Her chest hurt, and the breath rasped in and out her mouth, coppery-tasting, flooded with saliva. Tass rolled over in the broken fronds and threw his arms out, laughing.

"We're—almost—there," he panted, sitting up, "almost—to Mossy Creek. That's what my old man—calls it."

The odd thing, she later thought, was that even when they arrived, she could not see the place. Closer, closer: still, she could not make it out, even when a child's voice cried out Tass's name. It wasn't until she crossed a stream and almost bumped into the house that she at last saw the shingled roof sheathed in moss and the porch, half-hidden behind the sprawling rhododendron bushes that the Adantans called laurel, even though they weren't moun-

tain laurel at all. Out of the shadowy passage between the shrubs poured children of every age, tod-
dlers and others old enough to go to school, some
half-grown and others nearly men and women.
Tass's mother followed them, wiping her hands on
an apron and bounding up the bank as lightly as a
child. Shy, Adanta tried to hold back, but Tass
gripped her hand, towing her straight into a pack of
jumping little ones. They took her in, pawing at her
dress, pointing and laughing at the bob-tailed bird at
her back, calling out her name while Tass repeated it
for one and then another until his mother came up
and, as if parting the waters, pushed open a path.
Scolding, she threw her arms around her son and
rocked him to and fro; in the next moment she held
him at arm's length and, noticing the stranger,
hugged the two together.

Adanta liked that, that the mother accepted her
immediately.

An instant later she was trying to take in the names
and fasten them to faces: Will, who was tall and lean
with long black hair, quite grown up, born next after
the dead brother, Rob; Sylva, the oldest girl, quick
and pretty; her younger sisters—Sasa, who looked
about fifteen and could not stop laughing and Tewa,

a girl younger than Adanta, who was now busy springing from the porch to the ground and back again; Kephart, a solemn boy of perhaps seven; Whittier, about four years old but dressed only in a shift; Dills, a round-headed toddler, who was trying to copy Tewa by hopping from the bottom step and then climbing laboriously back up; a red-faced and howling baby they called Mullygrubs. When Adanta confessed that she couldn't possibly remember so many names, Tass's mother Moonie only smiled.

"And that's only one of their names each," she said, surveying her brood.

Before long they were all sitting around a summer fire while supper boiled in the pot, and the two travelers by turns told the saga of how Adanta had left home and found Magpie Joe and Caledonia and Tass and of what had happened at the Pony Fair. She could tell they were used to good storytelling, because they were silent and hushed in the right places, only a few sighs and low remarks between Will and Sylva punctuating the part of the story where she told how the Lean One had stolen her mother away. When Tass recounted how they had searched for the Teller of Wonders and found Lalu, Moonie and the older children talked all at once, telling Adanta what a piece of luck it was, what a rare thing it was to meet with one of the Yunwi Tsunsdi. And to have one know your name! Not much else about the latest Pony Fair surprised them, for they had all—even Whittier, Dills, and Mullygrubs—made the journey there and back in the past week. That they were well acquainted with Magpie Joe and Caledonia she could also tell, from the way the older ones roared as she told about her first meeting with him.

"We all love the man and Caledonia, too," Moonie said, wiping her eyes, "or we wouldn't laugh so hard."

"That Joe's a cutup," Will added, "he sure is. Like nobody else."

"Oh, I don't know." Sylva leaned over to tap her forehead gently on the table, setting Sasa to giggling, harder and harder until her mother got up and put a hand on her shoulder.

Adanta liked how Moonie looked—quick to smile, bright-eyed, and childish in her thinness, appearing far too small to have produced such a bumper crop of children. And maybe more, she guessed, remembering the cross at the rockslide. Moonie and the girls wore dresses much like her own, tight at the waist but full-skirted and topped by aprons—

Moonie, Sasa, and Tewa in russet gowns, Sylva in indigo blue. The mother was, like little Dills, plump-faced, with big eyes but a small nose and mouth. She had a good manner with the older children, getting them to jump about and help with the work—supper was steaming on the board table only minutes after she stirred the kettle a final time and declared it "done." With their fresh mountain appetites, the children polished off several bowls of mush and a salad of stewed greens, all the time talking and telling stories.

"Ma," Tass said, standing up, "where's Daddy?"

She shrugged.

"Gone, Tass. As bad as you to be wandering. Roy's gone off to some old woman in the Lands Beyond who grows the best long-necked gourds. Before he comes home again, he'll be trading a fiddle to a fellow for some dry walnut, and then it's a morsel of hickory he's wanting. It'll be a time before he's back, I reckon."

"Maybe not so long," Sylva put in, touching Tass on the arm as she passed by with another bowl of greens.

Sitting back down, the boy leaned toward his mother.

"Gourds and walnut and hickory: I guess he'll be making some banjos soon."

Moonie nodded, warming her hands around a cup of sassafras tea.

"I'm just cold all the time, even in the summer," she told Adanta. "Always have been. I should've been a foreigner, down in the swamps and flatlands where the alligators and fire ants and such heat-loving monsters roam about, looking for prey."

After the lamps were lit, she started to get the children, one by one, ready for bed. Once the five youngest children had been washed in a tub by the fire, the others undressed and bathed in an adjacent lean-to. Adanta was surprised by the way they piled, higgledy-piggledy, onto some ancient iron beds at bedtime—the little ones together with their mother, girls with girls, boys with boys. But no one here thought anything of it, nor of the way the beds were jammed together in the same chamber. Nor of the ceiling, hung with Roy's fiddles and banjos and mandolins, some in various stages of completion.

For a long time after the others she stayed awake, looking about the room with its unpainted boards and at Sylva's face, close beside her own and lit by a beam of moonlight. She was lovely, almost doll-like in the regularity of her features, the delicate shape of her brows, the shining hair. Awake, however, she was certainly no china figure. Just before dressing for bed she had chased Tass through the house onto the porch and wrestled him to the ground out in the yard, yelling, "Uncle! Say Uncle!"—all because he'd said she had a sweetheart and he meant to know who. Sylva had hollered to the others, watching from the front porch, "The only name he knows now is Uncle! That's my sweetheart."

Never had Adanta slept with so many people. It made her uneasy, and she sat up to look out the window.

"*Hist,*" a voice called. "Tomorrow we'll find Polk and bring him home."

She lay down again without speaking. Although she was weary from rough walking, her thoughts kept flittering from place to place. She remembered the witchmaster with his talk of Raven Mockers and caves, Lalu and the streaming fireflies, Mrs. Terrell and her tin tub. She listened to the breathing of the others, and it occurred to her that a person could be lonelier in a crowd than anywhere else. She remembered the canopy bed in her own bedroom in the Little Cottage In Between, empty and forlorn. Would Ba or Mama ever come in her room to say good night, or perch on the edge of the bed for a quiet talk? Would they three ever again be warm and comfortable sitting by the fireplace or around the table? She could almost feel her mother hovering over her in the dark, a kiss brushing against her forehead. Before the single tear caught in the corner of her eye could escape and slide onto her cheek, she fell asleep.

THE STOLEN BRIDE

The clouds were still snared in the laurel as Tass
and Adanta set out in the morning; early as they
woke, while Sasa and Tewa and Sylva slept, it was
not as early as Moonie, who was already hoeing in a
patch of beans—"greasy cut-shorts," she called
them—with Dills and Mullygrubs, dressed only in
long-tailed shirts, playing in the dirt at her feet. Nor
were they up in time to see Will, who had left before
dawn and would be gone all day. An expert stonema-
son, he tramped all over Adantis building walls and
chimneys. While the cabin at Mossy Creek was only
two rooms deep, four rooms in all, an impressive
chimney rose at one end, with squared cornerstones
and a wide mouth, a slate shelf for raising bread, and
a bake oven which Will had read about in a foreigner's book and copied. At the back of the chim-

ney, a horseshoe kept witches from sliding down the flue and into the house. When Adanta cast a backward glance as the trail began to rise, she could still make out the shaft of the chimney, although the rest of the cabin had melted into the shadow of trees. Above them the way to the Messers' camp lost itself in mist and rhododendron. Halfway up the mountain she heard a voice shouting, and soon Sylva burst into sight, her skirts gathered up in her hands as she leaped the trickles of water that crossed the path.

"Here," she panted, thrusting a sack at Tass. "I made it myself yesterday—you can't go off without food."

She flung her arms around the boy, squeezing him until he whooped.

"You take care, Tassel. And if things don't turn out the way you planned, well, it'll be all right just the same." Letting go, she stepped back, eyes intent on his.

"I'm not worried. By tonight I'll be riding Polk again." Tass grinned, and he looked his sister up and down. "I've never seen that gown. You're dressed mighty grand to be out for a run."

"It's Mrs. Terrell's weaving—white flax and wool mixed. I bought it with my own money. From raising turkeys last year. You like it?" Sylva shook out the skirts. The low-necked bodice showed her under-shift, edged with tatting—as was the hem that peeped from below the dress. Below the lacy border, her toes peeped out, bare and dirty.

He cocked his head to one side. "Wash your feet and comb your hair out, and you might just be the best-looking girl in the country."

Giving him a push, she turned to Adanta.

"Keep an eye on him. If he gets mad with the Messers, he could do most anything. And you," she added, poking a finger at his chest, "don't start a quarrel and make them feud with us, you hear?"

"Who cares," he retorted.

"I do. And you cared the time Rory and Darryl came and chunked up our old chimney, right in the coldest part of January, all because you kicked Harlan Messer in the shins. Don't you dare, no matter what." Hands on her waist, she defied him.

"Those big old boys," he scoffed. "I'm not afraid of them. But I won't bother the Messers. I'll just get what's mine and hightail it out of there. As for Harlan, he's nothing but a Messer runt. He can't be more than about six feet and five inches."

"Six foot nine is what I hear," Sylva replied, "and I believe that's just about tall enough to whip a shirt-tail boy."

"Don't you call me a shirttail boy," he warned, shoving her against the trunk of a pine. "You take that back."

Sitting down to watch the show, Adanta reached in the bag and pulled out the loaf. Breaking off a piece, she began to eat it slowly so as not to waste a bite.

The two siblings were sparring, thrusting against one another, hand to upraised hand.

"You're not a shirttail boy," his sister panted.

At that, Tass jumped backward; he snatched the bread from Adanta's lap and tore off a portion.

Smoothing her skirt, Sylva watched him stuff a strip of crust into his mouth before she added: "I just said that because I didn't want you to mess up my new gown."

"Whatever you say. Good bread, though."

"It's pretty tasty," his sister conceded. She took several pins from her bodice and began fastening up her skirts. Adanta thought that she looked very pretty, even with mud-splashed feet and her hair all in a tumble.

"Farewell, then," Sylva said, looking so serious that Tass laughed out loud.

"I'll be back tonight."

"I know. Just be careful, will you? I'll miss you." She leaned over and gave him a kiss, right on the lips, then laughed and skipped away, down the steep path.

The boy stared after her.

"There's something not right," he murmured, and even after they started up the hill, he paused several times to look back.

Toiling over the mountains, Adanta grew warm and longed for her T-shirt and jeans, which she had left for Kephart when he grew big enough for them. Even in Adantis, one occasionally saw blue jeans, although only on boys and men.

Whenever they stopped, she let White Brow out of the cage and sat down to watch her antics. Magpie Joe had been right: the injured bird seemed to have no trouble hunting in the leaves and weeds on the forest floor. Tass, on the other hand, was not as much company as usual. He was silent most of the time, and she wondered whether he was thinking about his sister or about the giants, who might well be dangerous if they were roused.

When they halted to eat, Tass picked at the bread, tossing crumbs onto the trail.

"I told a lie—told Ma we were only going to scout," he confessed. "Now I'm pondering if maybe that's all I should do. What I was thinking was that it would be easy to get Polk—you could wait—and afterward we could ride to your grandmother's place in the laurel. Or try to find it. That's why I said to bring your pack and the bird, so we wouldn't have to return to Mossy Creek, but maybe we should."

He flicked a piece of crust to a chipmunk. "If I take a look around, perhaps I can come back in a day or so with Will . . . It seemed so simple, last night. Like a game."

Adanta remembered the knob on Polk's forehead, like the ghost of a unicorn's horn. She felt glad that Tass had planned to go on with her as far as Birdie Ann's place and wondered if she could have found the way alone, not knowing the mountains as he did.

"But you don't want to put it off," she reminded him.

"No. Polk might be sold by then. And Sylva told me that she'd heard the Messer men would be off carousing today—so I'd have nothing to worry about but the women. Although I'd hate to get them storming after me."

"Well, why don't you decide when you get there?"

"It would be bad if something went wrong," he muttered, "and I had told Ma a lie."

Adanta stood up, slipping on her pack.

"It won't hurt us just to see, will it?"

Although Tass had claimed to be near neighbor to

the Messers, it was almost three hours before they reached the outskirts of the summer camp. Scaling an outcropping of granite and wind-blasted trees that brooded over the hollow where the Messers had chosen to build their cabins, the two crept from tree to laurel to scrub.

"Seems like the men are all gone," Tass whispered.

From their vantage point on a ledge of stone, Adanta could see eight big cabins in a cluster. Set apart from the others was a newer house, two stories high, with a wide porch circling the lower story.

"That's pretty." She pointed to the one by itself. Out front the flowers rioted inside a picket fence, and someone had set up a millstone for decoration.

Tass grunted.

She guessed what he was thinking: that it wasn't like a Messer to have a neat yard or flower beds or a home that looked like something other people might want to live in.

"They could have built right on top of a cave, couldn't they? But they have to be able to get the horses in and out." The boy scanned the ground, the boulders strewn along a crag, the nearest mountains.

"Maybe we should just start searching the woods."

But they didn't have to hunt long. As Adanta hopped from a ledge, one leg plunged into the ground up to the thigh. A single shriek flew from her mouth before she clapped a hand to her lips. Tass spun around, his eyes staring at empty air.

"Here, here," she called, waving.

Dropping the near-empty sack, he flew to her side, grabbing her below the arms and tugging.

"Don't," the girl cried out. She could feel shards and dirt grating on the skin as far as her knee.

Pausing, Tass examined the ground and tried to work his hand into the gap. "You're good and stuck," he admitted.

"Something's creeping up my skin." Her voice rose. "Something's crawling on me." Seizing his shirt with both hands, she stared into his face.

"Kick. Maybe it's nothing. Maybe bats or spiders if it's the roof of the cave. Sssh, quiet, quiet. Just kick. Kick hard," he told her, but she shook her head.

"I can't move it to kick—just my foot." Adanta thought she might scream.

Tass stared at her, then stood up and grasped her under the arms again. He jerked her upward, wrestling the limb from the narrow shaft. Scraped and red, it twisted free almost to the kneecap. There it lodged.

"No, stop, slow down, stop," she hissed, gripping

on to his arms. Trilling, White Brow sang with excitement. Adanta groaned. She shut her eyes. Now he was bending over the hole; his hands were circling her leg. It seemed to Adanta that the knee might fly to pieces, might be cut in half by a spear of stone. Suddenly it budged, slid along rock, and shot upward, the lower leg and foot banging against the walls of the crevice. As she collapsed onto moss and leaves, the girl could see blood trickling over her ankle.

Pulling up her skirt, she saw that the knee was cut, already discolored—mottled and reddish purple. Maybe it was broken. Dumping the bread out on the grass, Tass began to tear the bag into strips until Adanta rummaged in her pack for the knife her mother had left behind on the window seat. Methodically he cut the cloth into bandages, then bound them about the injured joint.

"What a fool I was to be so rough." He struck himself on the forehead with the palm of his hand. "Now I need Polk more than ever."

"Don't worry. It's done," she said faintly, trying not to weep. Feeling nauseated, she lay back in the grass and weeds. The sunlight struck her face, and she fixed her attention on the heat and the glow that came through her eyelids, but it was no use. The wound ached terribly. Tass decided the treatment was all wrong, that she needed cold water on the leg, so then there came an awful bumping piggyback ride down to a stream. There she sat with her knee submerged in a shallow rapids until the skin burned and she could no longer bear the numbness in her feet. Meanwhile Tass collected her pack and the bird and started hunting for a door to the cave.

About thirty minutes later he reappeared.

"How's the leg? I've found a gap. And there's not a soul in sight. Can you walk?"

Despite what had happened, Adanta wanted to see the pony robbers' hideout, but it was not until Tass borrowed the knife again and cut her a fresh staff—oak, this one was—that she managed to stand. The throb of pain was worse than she had imagined it would be. Still, between the boy and the staff, she hobbled along. The leg hurt so much that her face bloomed with sweat and she had to ask Tass to wipe it away, which he did, very gently. The secret entrance was not what she had pictured. It was just an irregular hole in the rock, but big enough for a horse to pass through. The chamber inside was choked with rubble, although a passageway had been cleared. Gray stalactites hung from the roof, where she could make out some long-legged spiders and a clump of tiny bats. Farther on, a higher chamber could be seen. By light from a fissure in the roof she glimpsed a few pink stalactites fastened to the ceiling. As she watched, a great tear rolled heavily down the side of one and plummeted to the floor.

"I want to go—up there," she whispered. The two crept along the wall, one hanging on to the other.

As they climbed, Adanta held out a hand and let a milky drop splash on her fingers. It was icy. She shuddered as she heard the noise of clumping footsteps from farther on. Pressing themselves into a corner, Tass and Adanta waited. The pulse of blood in her knee seemed to grow more pronounced with each approaching step.

"Hurry up, Iola," an annoyed voice boomed, echoing on the passageway.

"I coming, I coming, Queewee." The reply was sweet and loud, a small child's tones.

Preceded by her shadow, an immense girl thumped past, red plaits flopping, arms and legs bursting out of a too-tight dress. As she passed, the irritated young giantess kept repeating, "Hurry up, hurry, hurry," but she didn't bother to check on Iola, whose stumpy cast shade came into view, wobbling along the wall. Adanta breathed shallowly through her mouth, her eyes brimming with water from the strain of standing on the hurt leg, and she gasped a little as the child lurched into the candlelight and peered around. A crinkled aureole of hair stood out from her head, with its big saucer stare and red mouth.

Catching sight of a stranger, she crowed a greeting and stamped forward, making Adanta moan as she tugged at the gown and braided belt.

"Kiss," the toddler chortled, her command ringing on stone.

"Do it," Tass begged.

The girl bent and kissed Iola's cheek.

"Fah," she exclaimed, as the child swayed down the hall, calling, "Queewee, wait me."

Leaning against Tass, Adanta wiped her face on his shirt.

"Giant's drool," she gasped.

"Not on me!" He thrust her away, and she let out a squeak. "Sorry, really sorry, I didn't mean to hurt you."

"Did you see the straw on her clothes?" Adanta whispered. "The horses must be here."

"Should I leave you? But I'm afraid they'll come back and carry you off somewhere—you'll have to come, if you can." Uncertain, he peered down the passageway. They could still hear Iola babbling to her Queenie.

Tass half carried, half dragged Adanta up the slanting ramp. Warmth and the odor of horses pressed against them, a dense cloud.

He clicked his tongue and called, "Polk . . ."

The pony whickered, trotting toward them. Nine or ten horses milled about in the chamber, neighing softly at this new disturbance. Leaving Adanta propped against the wall, Tass groped about in the gloom. With a lunge he forced back the bars of a rude gate.

"Come on, boy, come on." Polk was all over him, nuzzling his neck, rubbing up against his face. "Hush, hush. It's Adanta, see, she's here in the dark, but she's hurt. And you have to carry us, so hold still a minute." Rocking his head as if he understood, the horse waited, hide twitching, while Tass struggled to help the injured girl.

"It's too easy," the boy muttered, "it's been dead easy. Something's wrong, something . . ."

Adanta didn't care. All she could think about was getting away and lying in a clean bed, preferably by herself. With a yelp, she at last swung the bad leg over Polk's back and pulled up her grandmother's birth gift, White Brow hooked to one side. Tass leaped on behind, kicking the horse with his heels so that Polk scrambled down the ramp and rapidly picked his way through the rubble of the first chamber, before bolting out the door. An avalanche of ponies and horses followed, flowing out of the cave into the sunshine, where they whinnied in gladness.

Iola's prattle became a scream.

"My powees, my powees, my powees," came the heartbreaking roar. Sluggishly Queenie turned and began to protest. In the compound a number of huge women materialized on porches and began to holler, one sprinting with thunderous footsteps toward the wails of Iola while the others stampeded toward the horses, which were now dodging here and there, swerving in panic.

"Yah, yah, Polk," Tass shouted, kicking the pony hard, and Polk dived straight down the mountain, toppling through rhododendron and ferns, plunging in a frantic bid for escape. Behind them the other horses cried out, rearing, bucking, each pitching in a different direction from the lip of the clearing. On all sides the laurel hells burst open and horses leaped and belly-flopped onward, downward, any way that was away from the cave, the spiraling howl of Iola's inconsolable voice, and the angry faces of the giant women.

Much later, when Adanta tried to recall that flight back to Mossy Creek, all she could remember after they had dropped from the edge of the Messers' clearing was an endless green galloping waterfall, the warmth of Tass leaning over her, and their heads low to the pony's mane as gravity pulled Polk on, his hooves barely touching the earth.

Even what came afterward was a blur, although she could remember Tass's face in hers, her own voice protesting that she felt fine, the leg was better, that she could walk or run or ride. She clung to him, determined not to be unfastened; then at once they were back at the cabin. The clearing churned with movement: horses neighed and whickered, eager to be off. Many red-haired men, some with beards like burning bushes and some pink and clean-shaven, were shooting their guns into the air, while Moonie scolded from the porch and Sasa and Tewa shrieked and the littlest children sobbed. Adanta caught a glimpse of Sylva, her face half-laughing, half-alarmed, seated astride a jet-black stallion, riding pillion behind a tall black-haired man, just before the whole party wheeled, pounding off in a fog of dust. She remembered Tass's screaming that it was all a plot, a plan to get him out of the way because he was the man when his daddy and Will were gone—and he was blaming the witchmaster, protesting that now he knew why the old man had said he might get his pony back but lose something he valued more, that it was all a trick from beginning to end. Then he was whooping, "Yah, yah, Polk," as Moonie scolded him and said to put the girl down and stay, stay, that it wasn't, wasn't what he thought, not exactly, but Tass paid no heed. Polk rocketed out of the yard, later slowing in his climb to the Messer compound because he was, after all, a pony, however sturdy, and no match for the great stallions and mares of the Messers.

After that, in Adanta's memory it was all a dark nothing except for the bright sun-throb in her leg until she jerked up her head because Tass was raising a rebel yell; somehow she felt no surprise to see that Polk was surging through the center of the Messers' summer camp amid a herd of laughing giants, who were firing their guns again in celebration, and she saw Iola, beet-faced, puffing on a whistle with all her might. When Polk cantered up to the door of the ninth house, the one with the flowers and the millstone, they sailed right around the cabin and back again, as Tass clamored for his sister. Sylva came out on the porch with the black-haired man who was tall but not so gigantic as the other Messers—just plain tall and as handsome with his black hair and blue eyes as she was pretty, so that it seemed they belonged together. The brother and sister, Tass and Sylva, argued as the crowd hullabalooed until all at once the first star of evening appeared, and there was a hush in the rumpus like an angel passing over. In the quiet, everyone could hear White Brow trilling like mad and Sylva hurling an answer at her brother: "I love him and I'm going to have him, and I'm not coming home again. Everybody in Adanta knows I love Harlan Messer, everybody but you, Tass, so just stay for the wedding because they've nabbed a preacher, too. The whole world's been fetched and is on the way, even Daddy to play the fiddle for reels, so stop, stop it, Tass." At which the Messers all huzzahed and made a ruction—their menfolk popped off their guns and the children rang bells or blew whistles and the noise of it all roared in Adanta's head until it was louder than the beating in her leg, and she wavered on the horse, seeing a green and black confetti of specks in the air. Then suddenly she fainted dead away, tumbling off Polk and plummeting down a dark and trilling green waterfall of leaves mixed with the tails and heads of horses.

THE EYRIE

"Day after day it was just the same. The air picked up a savor, like the smell of sweet shrub in bloom. It swirled with honeyed songs. By the ninth day the people could make out the words, warning them. Though this was long before the Cherokee were lashed from their homes and forced west on the march out of Adantis and the Lands Beyond, when so many died, the voices spoke of coming trouble. Sasa, your ancestor Tsikilili was just a child, playing in the dirt. All over the mountains the people started to fast and pray when the Nunnehi's call grew strong. A week later the Nunnehi flew to some of the people and carried many of them away, lifting up whole townhouses. Tsikilili lived on the Hiwassee River near Shooting Creek, and she was so young that she only looked about with curiosity when the chanting told about hard years to come. But her mother and father and all those people in the Cherokee village prayed for the Nunnehi to bring them out of the flittering, changing world and into the still, eternal places. When the Nunnehi arrived, the people by Shooting Creek were glad, hurrying into the deep hollows of the Hiwassee. The leaping stream shut over their heads. Tsikilili laughed in surprise as the people followed the immortals down, and she gripped her mother's skirt. As they approached the riverbank, the child remembered the doll she called Lalu, made from a white deerskin and stitched with beads of bone. She turned and hurried back to her play place in the laurel. Too late her mother saw and begged her to hurry. Then she dipped her head under the current, following Tsikilili's brothers and sisters.

"As she grasped the doll, the child heard a thunder of crashing waters. When she reached the river, the surface was restless, with no sign of her people or of the Nunnehi. She tried to follow, but the foam stung her nose when she breathed it in, and the waves knocked her back onto the shore.

"She sat down and cried on the banks of the Hiwassee, because she remembered her mother and all the people. Young as she was, the child knew they were gone forever."

"And that's the end. You told it just like Daddy." Sasa sounded pleased.

Adanta had been half listening to the tale, and only now that it was finished did she feel strong enough to open her eyes. It was shadowy in the room, which smelled of fresh-cut pine. She could hear White Brow chirp, *kep-kep, kep-kep.*

"There. She's awake," said the storyteller's voice.

Gazing toward the windows, Adanta saw Moonie with Mullygrubs asleep on her lap, Sasa at her feet. After putting the baby down in an oversized cradle and telling her daughter to go outside with the other children, she stood up, shaking out her apron.

"A mite better?" the woman asked, leaning over the bed.

The girl stared, not taking in the words.

"How's your leg?"

It lay under the coverlet like a stone.

"All right," she whispered.

Moonie pushed the damp hair back from the girl's forehead. "The swelling's going down, but it looked pretty sore last time I checked. You missed the shooting and all. The Messers, they whooped it up after the wedding. What a ballyhoo! The supper was fine, and those big old boys just kept playing steal-the-shoe. That's an old Adantan wedding game. Stealing Sylva's shoe right off her foot from under the table. They are wild, those Messers. Just fighting and drinking shine and partying all evening. Sheer devilment. One group kidnapping her and Harlan, just in fun. The others robbing them back. Those are old, old Adantan ways. Then it was just one jig or reel after another until time for bed."

"How long was I asleep?"

"Well, after Red Betty Messer gave you a sleeping draft, you slept about two days, off and on. Every once in a while we got you up."

"I don't remember."

"No, I don't guess you do. That boy Tass got the jawing of his life for galloping over the mountains—and you with a bad knee. I believe he thought his mama and daddy wouldn't ever quit telling him about his own pure foolishness. He won't forget that talking-to for a while."

"I didn't mean to get him into trouble . . ." Adanta rolled over on her side, wincing as the leg shifted.

"Nobody got him in trouble but his own self." Moonie sat down on the edge of the bed.

"Where am I?"

"Why, you're in my daughter Sylva Messer's back bedroom, here on the mountain with these giants. They're out gallivanting, still celebrating the wedding. It'll probably be a week before they're done gadding about. Never did I think a daughter of mine would marry a Messer. Be a Messer. But if it had to happen, Harlan would be the one to wed. He's tall enough, but you wouldn't call him a *Tsunil kalu*. And he's just about the only one without that red devil hair. They'll have a brood of handsome children someday, sure enough."

Her eyes moved across the room.

"He's not like most of the others. He's a good worker, a hard worker. This is a right pretty house, and he cut the trees, notched the logs, did all the finishing work."

She paused, her head bent.

"I reckon it's meant to be, Harlan and Sylva. Makes me feel old, having a daughter married."

"Where's Tass?"

"He'll be coming by soon. He feels bad about your leg, about getting carried away."

Each hour that passed in Sylva Messer's new cabin pressed on Adanta, reminded her that she had somewhere else she needed to be. Much of the day she spent alone, dozing in the big back bedroom. Occasionally she heard singing or laughing from another part of the house. Once a day Tass came over to bring the news from Mossy Creek. And each morning Red Betty swept into the room, jerking back the coverlet to examine the swollen knee. Enormous and untidy, she roared out her verdict: "It's bad still, you hear?" Red Betty's brats waited for her outside, their noses squashed against the windows. Then silence returned to the room.

In the quiet of the mountaintop, Adanta recalled her adventures. In memory she fled to the Little Cottage In Between, where for precious minutes she and Ba and Mama lived together, safe behind blue window frames, with no strange visitors from the mountains. One afternoon she hoisted her pack from the floor and spilled its contents across the coverlet. Drawing the stole across her legs, she felt comforted. The knee would heal, and she would walk the Adantan world and find her grandmother, Mama, Ba. Her hand brushed the cloth binding of the book given by her grandmother. "What use you make of it—that is up to you," Birdie Ann had said. Fanning the pages open, Adanta saw the flecks in the handmade paper. It still looked as if words seethed just below the surface. That afternoon, when she asked for something to write with, Tass brought her an ancient-looking steel pen and a bottle of golden-brown ink.

Flipping to the back of the volume, she began writing an Adantan dictionary, scribbling down all the words and plants and names she could think of—everything that belonged to Adantis. When in doubt, she flipped through Harlan Messer's own copy of Mooney, an Adantan printing of James Mooney's *Myths of the Cherokee*. It, along with the author's *Sacred Formulas of the Cherokees*, ran to six letterpress volumes, each bound in handwoven fabric. The evening and the next day's morning hours slipped away, until a visit broke into her labors. Even then she fired questions at Moonie about people and stories and the old days: Was she really named for James Mooney? Why were giants from the west? Wasn't bride-stealing bad? The older woman declared that "somebody sure must be feeling better to ask such a heap of questions." Later, alone again, Adanta took up the book, running her hands over the flecks as if they were a braille she might learn to read. Another day passed before she again dipped the steel pen into the homemade ink. Uncertain what to write, she dried it on a rag and laid it down. Closing her eyes, she imagined the cardinal flowers in the garden before the Little Cottage In Between, a Pony Boy whose name she did not yet know, the spring-leaf color of the Corn Woman in the maze, the smell of corn mush, a smear of dirt on a forehead, fireflies tossed from a smoke hole, a sleeping face by moonlight. Such fragments of past days awakened her completely. She wanted to make something new—a something as lovely as the thin green shuck that wrapped its warmth around her legs, as strong as the cabin that Harlan Messer had made out of love for Sylva, as busy with character as the kitchen table back home, its oval bordered with carvings of mountain animals.

When she unstoppered the bottle of ink once more, Adanta was dreaming of the wilderness, the folded ridges that are often the shade of twilight. The image in her mind shaped itself into words, meeting and matching with the flecks in the page as if the story were already half written. She remembered one of Moonie's stories about the Immortals, how the people who sank underwater with the Nunnehi still murmur beneath the waves. Sometimes they reach up from the depths and catch hold of a fisherman's net, just to let those living on the land remember that their old relatives are still busy below the surface. So it was with her words. They poured out like a flood from the water carrier's jar, and the flecks on the page rose to float on its buoyant current. Quickly they spread into chapters as she retraced the path from the Little Cottage In Between to the Pony Fair and Mossy Creek and the summer place of the giants.

On the twelfth day, Red Betty pronounced the leg to be on the mend and said she could now bathe, and that she could try to walk about in a day or two. That afternoon, when Tass arrived, a pet flying squirrel on his hat to amuse her, she was dressed in her mulberry-colored gown. Although she admired the bright-eyed creature, Adanta didn't want to watch its antics. She insisted that Tass cut her a hiking staff to replace the one she had lost when they rescued Polk from the cave. Then, gripping his arm and the stick, she hobbled out into the sunshine, gritting her teeth against the pain. It wasn't as bad as she had expected, but it was there, a dull pulse. In a moment she stood alone, with only the crutch for help.

"I can do it," she told him. "Where's Polk?"

Tassel had seated himself on the grass and was now watching her clumsy steps. Without making an answer, he pulled his long hair back and bound it with a string of wool.

"Where's Polk?" she repeated.

"He's around front. Wandering. I don't even have to tie him now that the Messers are in-laws. Did I ever tell you that they didn't steal him to get me out of the way? Nobody even thought of it. They just plain old robbed me. Didn't even care that Harlan was going to kidnap my sister. Stole from their own future kin and didn't bat an eye. Anyway, he's loose. Probably grazing on Sylva's blossom bushes."

"Go get him."

"Why?" Tass broke off a stem of grass and started chewing on it.

Adanta leaned against the porch railing.

"You did say that you'd go with me as far as my grandmother's, didn't you?"

"I will, but you don't want to ride Polk like—"

"I need him, Tass; can't you see? Let's get out of here."

"What about your knee? Mama will tan my hide if I go dragging you over the mountains."

"I'm choosing to go. I need to. I want to. I've lost too much time already."

Grinning, he shook his head.

"They'll skin me, for sure. You haven't even met my daddy. He's got an arm like a slat of hickory."

Adanta considered; it was true that she didn't know what had gone on with Tassel since the moment she had fallen from the horse. There might be things she didn't, couldn't fathom right now. Reasons for him not to come along. But her leg felt better, and it might be that movement and stretching would make it better still. It was hard to say. Stumping back inside the house, she lifted her pack from the bed and hooked White Brow's cage into place. The wren chirped once, then let out a trill, as if in encouragement.

Flat in the grass, the boy looked up at her, giving a one-sided smile.

"Where do you think you're going?"

Adanta pointed to the western mountains.

"*Ku!* You wouldn't make it over the first rise like that. Well, I guess I'm just doomed to a whipping. Unless it makes a good enough story. That's my daddy's weakness. A Teller can't help but love a tale." He sprang from the grass and let out a piercing whistle, and in a moment Polk rounded the corner of the cabin, ears pricked, mouth dripping with flowers.

"I've got an idea—I'll just leave this fellow for Sylva." Tassel sailed the hat with its bright-eyed rider into the back bedroom and closed the door.

Not a soul saw them go; even Iola was out of sight, napping in gigantic slumber. Or maybe most of the Messers had gone back to the farm, the girl speculated. However it was, she was glad to be left in peace.

It was pleasant to be off again, her arms around the pack, White Brow jumping and trilling in Caledonia's cage. Tass set the pony to a leisurely pace. Adanta felt comfortable, glad to be out in the world, and though the leg still ached, she was ready to ignore it. As they pushed slowly westward on winding trails, they met no one, not until midafternoon, when they spotted a figure ducking through some laurel.

"We must be close." Adanta lowered her voice to a whisper. "Though I never saw the graveyard with shells that Mrs. Terrell talked about."

"Well, I'm lost," Tass told her. "Never came here in my life."

They could hear whoever it was murmuring, occasionally laughing, although there seemed to be no second person.

"Can you tell us the way to the weaver's house?" Adanta called.

A burst of silvery notes answered her—strange, melodious warbles.

"To the weaver Birdie Ann," she added.

"You want the Sprangly Place," a voice piped. "Where the paths are all in a sprangle, every which way, and the laurels, too, just as thick and sprangled. When you reach it, take the most narrow and crooked trace upward. Keep to that, and you will come to the eyrie." The advice ended with a mischievous, bell-like quaver that made White Brow trill for joy. A flash of pale skin and shaken hair showed in the laurel; then the glimpse was gone.

Tass put a hand on Adanta's shoulder. Turning, her fingers gripping Polk's mane, she looked at him and nodded.

"Was it her? Lalu?"

He stared at the tangled rhododendron where the girl had shown herself for one glimmering instant.

"Ssshh. Maybe. The Yunwi Tsunsdi sometimes come to lost people. Lalu? I don't know," he whispered.

They pressed forward in the same direction, hoping that they were on course to the Sprangly Place. The track narrowed as it rose, twisting around rocks and trees. Streams jetted and splashed over stones, glittering like diamonds in patches of sun, gleaming and velvet-edged under the balsams. The air grew colder, sharper. Adanta tugged the stole from her pack and wrapped it around her body, first hooking White Brow's cage through a buttonhole of her dress. Huddled on the floor, the wren let out a single chirp. Although as warm and soft as ever, the surface of the weaving appeared changed in the thin air. The cloth glistened with a faint mist and here and there showed shades of blue. Tass shivered but said he was fine, didn't need any woman's shawl. Doubling back on itself, the path became steeper, clambering around huge ancient rhododendron, their gnarled stems rising high overhead. The leaves, Tass showed her, were beginning to bend downward and curl from the chill. In winter, he said, sometimes they would be furled, hanging dark and tight. The two rose through the laurel hells, higher, higher.

Sprangled, Adanta thought, seeing the many narrow waterfalls that wound and rushed impetuously over the stony ground. Whipped to foam, the water poured, flinging icy drops. The streams certainly appeared knotted, but it was a tangle of paths, not watercourses, that Lalu—if, indeed, it had been she—had predicted. Higher now, they were in a land where springs burst from the rock and sprayed downward.

"It's like the beginning of things," Tass shouted, draping an end of Adanta's stole across his back.

The laurel hells thinned out, the branches of rhododendron warped and bedeviled by years of wind. A gust blew their hair back and almost whipped the grandmother's stole over a precipice. Quick as a striking snake, Tass's hand snatched one corner and jerked. It flapped wildly, as if it were a captive that longed to be dashed downward, then to soar up into the freezing sky. White Brow struggled, chirping as she was thrown against the bars of her cage. The breeze shook frost into their bones. Up the pony struggled, to where the flowers shrank in size, their roots holding tenuously to pockets of dirt in cracks of stone. The frail blossoms fluttered, minute tethered kites, as the pony leaned into the rush of air and clouds bolted like panicky sheep across their way. When a misstep sent a shower of fragments down the trail, Tass jumped off and walked with his arm around Polk's neck, urging him on. Blasts of crystalline air buffeted the climbers, and Tass lowered his head against the thrust that raked his hair and clothes. A rut, then another, crossed their own. A few steps more and corkscrewing paths broke off in every direction.

Tass paused, staring at the maze of trails.

Adanta opened her mouth and called out, "the Sprangly Place," but the powerful wind stole her words and skated them off a mile or more, then let them drop.

"Which one?" he mouthed, and she twisted on the

pony's back, studying the loops and doublings-back. She counted seven paths "sprangling" upward, but there was one, almost invisible, that seemed more crooked and confused than the others.

"That one," she cried.

As the pony clambered on, Tass guiding his feet on the dim trace, Adanta glimpsed a huge raven, hurled by the wind. Yet it did not land or fly away into the cover of laurel or a lone twisted tree. It kept fighting the wind, which now and then won the tussle and catapulted the bird away. Each time it returned, dipping and veering, seeming to enjoy the wrestle. It dawned on Adanta that this creature, like the one in the corn maze, was guiding her onward. *Cr-r-uk*, *cr-r-uk*, it called to her. She pointed it out to Tass, who eyed the raven warily.

At last, crossing a ledge of rock, they found before them a big cabin set into the stone, its porches skirting the edge of an abyss. A forest of wind-twisted rhododendron and trees crowned the rock face behind the house and provided some shelter from the wind. The raven made a cry and dived through an open casement. After a few moments, a hand reached up and forced the window shut.

"I don't like this," Tass shouted, but still he led them on.

When the grandmother stepped onto the front porch, the wind slammed the double doors all the way open behind her, catching her black shawl and tossing it out like a pair of wings.

Fear like a claw swept along Adanta's spine.

"Grandmother, you are—" She broke off, alarmed by the words weaving in her mind, but Tass finished the cry. His hand grasped her arm, and his face was in hers as he shouted, "Adanta, Adanta, look, don't you see? Let's get out of here! This woman is a Raven Mocker—*a Raven Mocker*—whether you call her grandmother or not, she is, she can only be one of the Raven Mockers."

THE RAVEN MOCKER

In the whirling winds, Adanta, sliding from the horse, heard her grandmother's voice. She was addressing Tass.

"Don't be afraid. I have waited to hear those words for a very long time."

"Oh, no, no, no," Adanta called into the bursts of air, the witchmaster's words coming back to her, surging in her veins like sudden poison. *Speak out and name him . . . all his life and strength dribble away in seven days . . . You must not be afraid to speak, though he dies.* Hanging on to Polk, her leg aching as it had not ached in days, she stared at the old woman in the flapping shawl.

"Will you die now, Grandmother? Did Tass and I come all this hard way just to make you die?"

Her grandmother had not the least trace of sadness on her face.

"Don't be angry with your friend; promise me that, Adanta. No matter what happens. We find few enough who are true, whether we live in Adantis or in the Lands Beyond. Come inside, both of you, and I'll tell you how I came to be as I am."

Although Tass still looked as if he would rather throw himself down the ridge, he did, after some hesitation, help Adanta hobble to the porch.

"If you lead the pony into the trees, you'll find a glade. It's surprisingly calm. There's even some grass for him to eat."

The boy did as the old woman said, guiding Polk up the cobble-strewn slope behind the cabin. Afterward they gathered around the fireplace in the main room. There were many long windows opening onto the porch, through which could be seen views of tortured trunks bent against the blast, scudding clouds, and range upon range of blue mountains softened by blowing mist. Taking White Brow from under her shawl, Adanta unlatched the cage and set the wren on the hearthstone.

"How pretty!" Birdie Ann clapped her hands. "I hardly ever see the wrens here. The air's too brisk for them."

After warming herself, the bird began to hop about, searching for insects. It seemed that she was making herself at home, trilling while she hunted. But when the grandmother's shadow fell upon her, White Brow panicked and made a flustered, one-winged flight toward Adanta.

"I like them and all the dainty creatures that flit and skitter through Adantis, but they don't like me," the old woman said. "They know. Not even a lizard or a toad wants to cross my shade."

The girl, who had been looking around uneasily, spoke up. "Where is your husband, Grandmother? Should we be afraid of him?"

"There's nothing to fear. Your grandfather is dead."

"My grandfather," Adanta repeated, glancing at Tass.

"Yes, he was Jess's father. Not the one I would have chosen, but father just the same. I told you to think of me as Great-grandmother because I looked so very old; I was not sure you would believe that I could be your ba's mother. Yet his father looked infinitely older. It is good that you never met. He was a cruel man, but he loved me—perhaps more than a good man might have done, even though I only once or twice made him happy."

My grandfather. My own grandfather. Adanta stared out the window, where the wind was striving against the cabin, shaking the window frames. "What happened to him?"

"He was doing his evil business, going to hunt among the Adantans. About ten days ago. He had sensed something—an injured or sick person, a faint odor of disease on the wind. And he had gone out in the guise of a raven, riding the downdrafts, sweeping along the mountaintops and the coves. Flying into a clearing, he took his natural form—that of an aged man. Soon afterward he heard laughing and was surprised by a party of men and women. It seems there had been a wedding a few days before, and they were still celebrating. The bride and groom caught his eye, a couple handsome and ripe with health, just the opposite of what he sought. One of the others, a big fellow brandishing a whiskey bottle, shouted to my husband, saying, 'You're nothing but a Raven Mocker, you wrinkled-up rag of a man.' The party roared with delight. They meant him no harm, but he felt a searing pain in his breast and knew that someone in that crowd of revelers had believed those words and recognized him for what he was. Turning, he caught the eyes of the pretty bride upon his face. He crept away into the laurel and lay there a long time, weak and helpless, before he could again take the form of a raven."

"*Ku!*" Tass exclaimed, his eyes on Adanta.

She stared back at him. Her thoughts, her feelings made a great "sprangle" in which she was now lost. But she was not angry at Tass or at the careless wedding party. Even if she had been Adantan-born, she could not have prevented what had happened. Perhaps Kalanu had been seeking *her*, scenting out her injury—perhaps he, all unknowing, wanted to steal years from his own grandchild. Or would he have known and held back? Or worse, known and not cared? She wouldn't ask, as it would be cruel to question her grandmother and let her guess what they suspected. Yet to see her grandfather, just once! It would have satisfied something in her, to view his face, its features fissured by the years—the not-yet-lived years of the sick he had stolen and made part of himself as a Raven Mocker.

Birdie Ann did not notice the boy's outcry or else chose to ignore it.

"He spent his last days flying, coasting on the currents, or else curled on his bed. He fasted and did not go to his stick-castle in the forest, with its platforms and coils of withies, where he had been accustomed to eat his tainted food. For I would never let

187

him bring meat into this house, which he built out of desire for me. On the seventh day after he had come across that party in the woods, he died. I found his body on one of the trails below the house, and I piled rocks around to make a cairn."

She leaned toward Adanta. "Yes, I will die. Already I'm waning. I welcome the change from this world to the one beyond, except that I leave you and Jess. There is nothing else to keep me. I've been weary of my life since the day the curse of the Raven Mockers fell upon it and overshadowed it forever."

Adanta buried her face in the soft comfort of the stole.

"Miss Birdie Ann." Tass held out a hand toward the old woman. "Tell us your story. How did these things come to be?"

The grandmother bowed her head. "I am no Teller," she said slowly; "I've been too unused to human speech. Yet I'll tell you.

"As a girl, I was said to be beautiful. Because I wore my hair parted in the middle, with auburn wings pulled back over my ears, they called me Birdie. That girl—she was full of hope, eager to weave cloth that would astonish all Adantis and sure that she would meet some man unlike the common.

Ku! The dreams I had! As fine and airy as a ring stole.

"One spring day while I was hoeing beans in the field, a horseman passed by on a great black charger. His gaze felt heavy on me. I looked up. From where I stood, he seemed strong and straight. His features were handsome. Curious, a little alarmed, I watched him depart, the hoe stilled in my hand. Another day he rode into the yard, his eyes searching the porch until he found my face. My father stopped playing his mandolin in mid-song. We all stared—he was such a fine-looking man but somehow frightening in his silence, his boldness. And when he spurred the horse and galloped away, the others looked at me without speaking. Weeks, months went by. Gradually I ceased recalling him to mind. I had my beaus, who came to our house in the evenings. My favorite was a boy named Carlisle. Oh, I loved to see him coming! He gave me a ruby ring that had been his grand-mother's. One Friday his mother sent word that he was sick and could not visit. I felt so sad that I walked down to the stream and sat there, listening to the water for a long time. It was only three days later that his family bade us to the wake: Carlisle was dead. Until then I hadn't realized how much I had cared for him. I can remember looking at his dead body laid out on a table, with a plate of salt and earth on his breast."

"Why?" Adanta asked.

"The salt represents the spirit; earth, the flesh.

"I walked through that cabin, wanting to be where Carlisle had been. Everything said 'death' to me. They'd pulled pewter dishes from the shelves, and the mirror on the parlor wall was draped with a black cloth. The hands of the clock were stopped at the hour of his death. I stayed up with the others, all night long. I heard the women talking about how a raven's *prrr-r-uk!* had been heard just above the house an hour before Carlisle died. Then I knew that the Raven Mockers had come to him and robbed him of his breath and the years that should have remained to him. That was a wretched thought, but it became more terrible to me later, after my marriage.

"You never saw someone mourn and take on the way I did then, after I had heard those women whispering about my man. And it was a long time before I quit crying for Carlisle, thinking about the sort of life we might have had. I put the ring away in a box of basswood he had made for me, but I used to sleep with it under my pillow. In the evenings I would lie in bed, trying to picture his profile, the exact shade of his hair—it was blond, not like the rest of the children in that family, who had black hair.

"A year later it happened. We were on the slope above the house—me and Mama, my brother, Watson, my sister, Sally, and my father—picking berries. The air was warm; the blueberry bushes were starting to color up for fall. Daddy was humming a hymn tune as we worked our way uphill. It was *Will the circle be unbroken by and by, Lord, by and by?* I looked up, and I saw the horse standing like a tower of black in the grove of trees above us. I recognized it at once. Then I saw the rider. The man stared at me, as he had before. I could not stir. Fright pinned me where I knelt, my hand in the blueberry leaves. He crashed down the hill like an avalanche, the stallion flinging rock and sparks, streams of dirt and pebbles sliding from its hooves. Snatching me up by one hand, the stranger dragged me onto the horse and spurred it onward so that blueberries sprayed from my pail, and in seconds we were past the house, with the screams of my mother and Sally and the shouts of Wat and my daddy fading behind us. That very day I was married, and he brought me to this house, which he had built for me over the previous year. At that time I did not even know where I lived, for this part of Adantis is little traveled, perhaps because it is a stronghold for wizards, and a spot where the Nun-nehi and the Little People are more often seen than any other place. I was afraid of the gusts of wind and of the heights and of the trollish creature who guarded the house in those days, warning me inside if I wandered. Out of fear I clung to the husband whom I did not love. Within a year our son, Jess, was born. Alone I delivered him, tied the baby's cord, did all that was needed. Afterward I wept because I wanted my mother, but I was glad and felt blessed by the baby's coming. I believe that if he had not been given to me, I might have thrown myself from the precipice. For Jess, I lived. To please me, he was baptized in this very house, with a quaking kidnapped preacher to perform the rite.

"There were things I did not understand about my husband. I knew that something was wrong, perhaps magical, about him. A wizard, an immortal, a ghost—I imagined a thousand different answers. Right from the beginning, I would not share meals with him. I feared it—feared some powder or potion would harm me. Nor would I let him feed Jess or carry him out of the house. When home, Jess's father would toss him so high that I held my breath. Often, when he was away, a large raven would circle the house, crying out so mournfully that I would have tears in my eyes as I hurried to fasten up the windows.

"Why didn't I let myself be taught by the legends of our people—why did I not see him for what he was and call out the name of Raven Mocker? All the rest of my life would have been different, had he died then, and other deaths might have been prevented. Bitterly I reproached myself when I came to know that such recognition had been his greatest dread. That was why he tried so hard to make me like himself, for one Mocker is harmless to destroy another in that way.

"In those years I ate nothing but corn mush and occasionally fruit or vegetables or dried beans, all brought up from the valley by my husband's servant. I washed and washed them, just to be sure. It's hard to be always careful. Vigilant. During the third year of our marriage, my husband slipped something into my bowl of corn. When I tasted the mush, I knew there was something evil in my mouth, and I spat it out, but it was too late. One bite of the apple in Eden caused a fall from grace and lost us the garden. So also for me and the taste of a dead man's heart. That night, after I had rocked Jess to sleep, I was ill, and the raven came and pecked on the window glass. It was my husband's servant who broke the pane and let him in. I was lying on the floor, scared and suffering. I never forgave Kalanu for what he did to me, nor for watching without pity as I became a raven for the first time, not knowing what was happening."

The grandmother pointed to a window. "Look: the glass that does not match the others, you see, the one that has turned amethyst in the sun? That's where the creature smashed the pane."

"Don't stop," Tass told her; "you were wrong. You *are* a Teller. Anyone is who has a story worth the telling." He moved closer, attentive to her every word.

The grandmother continued, her fingers picking nervously at her gown.

"The wing-sheaths ripped open my back. That was the start of the falling away from what is human. It was fearsome, the first time, though even now I do not alter my form with ease. The plumage sprouted, my bones grew hollow, my feet curled. No matter how much strange joy it may bring, the change is always terrible. The blood cools, and the alien heart thrums in the chest. It is an awful thing to see yourself lost in a wild shape, to feel your mouth grow so hard and fierce that no one would ever kiss it, ever again. Croaks spill from the throat, *crr-ruk! cr-r-uk! crrr-u-k!*

"I burst out the window, now flung wide. The wind, like a slingshot, tossed me toward Orion. I lost all sense of north and south, top and bottom, plummeting toward the burning stars. End over end, I dropped down, down, down as the fountaining air died away. Flailing my wings, cawing into a fresh breeze, I caught myself: I *flew*. And that is the only part of being cursed with this form that I can praise, for never in all my youth had I felt such trembles, such *all-overs* of the spirit. Riding the currents as the clouds crossed the Milky Way, sailing above the pinpricks of light that show where Adantans live, even losing the shape of Adantis and arrowing miles past the boundary line—these have been my life's only pleasures, except for my weavings and my hope for a realm beyond this one. Also, I have found peace in remembering my son, Jess, and you, Adanta."

Birdie Ann's eyes, gentle, without anything in them of a bird's wildness, rested on her granddaughter.

"That night I forgot myself entirely, playing with the wind—throwing myself at the moon in the sky as if it or I were a child's ball. Kalanu and I sported, chasing each other from tree to tree, sliding down the air, skimming the surface of water. For the first time I reveled in him. I cared for nothing except the joy of our flying and shooting down the cold waterfalls of the air. I did not remember my child sleeping in his bed or the distrust I had always felt for my husband. When I grew tired, I lit on the ground and teased some fox pups out of their den, biting their tails and jumping into the air when they pounced. It is wonderful to leap up and feel pinions beat the body into flight. As dawn struck the mist, I was hanging high over the mountains, watching all of Adantis waken under its light. It was then that memory tugged at me, and I soared higher, farther, until I could see the familiar landmarks of my old home—a certain toothed crag, a stone face with marks like tearstains from rivulets of water, a lightning-scarred tree. Kalanu followed me for a time, before sailing down toward a settlement, but I did not care. By then it was hours past sunrise. I flew on, aiming straight toward home. When I got there, my father and brother were harrowing our pocket-sized field, while my sister sat in the shade, weaving a basket. For a while I remained content to watch from a serviceberry tree. Where was my mother? I felt anxious, uneasy. Swooping toward the house, I peered in the windows. My mother's loom stood empty, and no one came when I pecked on the glass. As I flew, my wings quivered. I circled the family graveplot, lit on the raw unmarked grave inside the fence pales. My mother was dead! My daddy looked stooped and thin. My sister was a young woman with hair down to her waist; my brother, a big-shouldered man. I heard him shout, pointing at the graveyard. In my grief I flew to them, crying out, circling the patch of field, lower and lower. It must have looked like an ill omen to them. Wat scrabbled in the dirt for a weapon and flung it at me. I spoke to him with pent-up longing: *Crrr-u-k!* His first lob missed, but the next one found its mark, knocking me to the ground. He pounded toward me, another lump of fieldstone in his hand. I sprang into the air, fleeing from my own blood, my near kin.

"It took me hours to wing back to the eyrie, calling for my mother with my rough voice the whole way, letting the wind carry my grief across Adantis. My brother had knocked sense back into me with his blow. No one grows up in our land without learning the old tales about the Raven Mockers, how they, in-visible, gather at the bedside of the sick or dying to frighten and shake a body free of breath, adding years that should-have-been to their own lives—

stealing the heart by magical means, leaving no scar. Afterward the Mockers take the form of witch or wizard and roast the heart on a peeled stick, eating it in communion with one another. I knew what I was now. I knew what my husband was. I knew that when he had flown down to the settlement, he had gone in search of his prey. I knew he or his kind must have knelt at the side of my dear Carlisle. The feathers at my nape prickled as I pictured my mother on her deathbed, the shadow of pinions falling across her face. Shrieking into the gust, I flew faster. I was getting back to my son. He was all that remained to me, the only creature I might safely love. I had left him—without a human thought or care for harm— my Jess, a tiny child.

"When I arrived, the door was open. I flew from room to room, crying out for my boy. Plunging from the porch, I searched the precipices. There was no trace of my husband, who must have gone to his lair to sleep off the night's adventures. *Prruk, prrruk, prrr-u-k,* I cawed. The sounds were nothing like a name. Having scoured the mountain, I finally found Jess in a grove of twisted trees, fast asleep, his body chilled, tears dried on his cheeks. Rubbing his head with my own, I woke him and little by little walked him down to the house. He wanted to catch the pretty bird, and so I hopped away, setting my claws in the safest spots for him to step as I went. I called him to me with a metallic *tok! tok! tok!* 'Bird,' he answered, jumping behind me. When he finally squeezed me in his arms, the cabin's strong walls around him, I relaxed and the change came over me. It is a thing a child should not see, but I could not help myself. I was too young in the ways of the Raven Mockers.

"To my sorrow, the body that returned to me that morning was older than the one I had owned the night before. This is how it must be—though sometimes I wonder why my innocence did not defy all harm. Maybe it was already tainted by Kalanu's nearness. Why weren't those years simply added on to the end of my own life? I believe the Raven Mocker is doomed to show the mark of evil, and so all freshness is withdrawn and blighted. Purity is frail. Youth is perishable. Mine couldn't bear the touch of wrong, I suppose, the gain of years stolen from another, the unclean taste in my mouth. Nor could I mask the wrinkles and aging as my husband did, because I refused to learn sorcery and disguise. The change scared Jess. It horrified me. That afternoon, when Kalanu came to us, he showed himself for the first time in his true form. To me he seemed a thousand years old, his skin like the paths below the house, intricately sprangled with wrinkles. I turned my face to the wall and would not look. Such is the shape of a Mocker.

"Since the day he crashed down upon me, the life of the Raven Mocker has been my curse. I was always vigilant if your grandfather came into the house when food was being prepared. I never again sought out my old home or saw my brother and sister and father. Perhaps all of them are dead. Maybe I'm aunt and great-aunt, many times over. Never did I seek out the sick or the dying or take from anyone what it's forbidden to take. I felt no human touch on mine other than that of my husband—if he were still human—and of my son. But even Jess I did not touch when the time neared for him to go out into the world. There was also the child my husband occasionally brought to visit: his own godson, born to Raven Mockers, a boy whom he had pledged to see grow up as one like him."

"Grandmother," Adanta broke in, "the godson—"

The old woman's eyes traveled to the amethyst pane. "Yes," she said, "it's as you guess. My husband was godfather to the one you call the Lean One."

"Did you ever fly with him again? Why didn't you

go back to your own people? How did Adanta's father escape? Did—"

"What a lot of questions!" Birdie Ann looked at
Tass and smiled.

"His father is a Teller," Adanta informed her
grandmother.

"Well, that explains it, I suppose. He'll be one
himself someday."

"I hope so." Tass looked eager, and Adanta suspected that he was storing up Birdie Ann's words
for a future time, when he might impart wonders.
"Please don't stop, Miss Birdie," he added.

"Well, maybe I can answer your questions, at least.
For years Kalanu begged me to soar with him over
the peaks, to play and rejoice in our bird shapes together, but I would not. I was a grief to him because
I refused his gifts and because I saw what we were—
tinged with evil. And because I wouldn't make myself young and pretty by his arts, his own wrong was
always before him. Too, he had a bird's longing
to raise up fledglings with me, as well as a Raven
Mocker's wish to breed up a clan of monsters. These
things I also denied him.

"Always I feared contact, especially with the ill
or injured, feared an unclean desire beating in my

breast. I agonized that the Raven Mocker in me might, at any moment, overthrow the girl, the woman. When Kalanu pressed me to let him have our son, that he was old enough to taste man's flesh, I fled with our boy and lived in the wilds beyond Talatu Place for three years. In all that time Jess and I never embraced, because I feared my touch could awaken the Raven longing in him. The latter part of childhood is when, if kindled, it can leap into flame and burn up the better life that came before. And when Jess became a young man, I sent him to the Lands Beyond, hoping that Kalanu would not find him, and I returned to my place on the mountain. Although my husband beat me for the first time when I came back, I didn't care: our son was safe in the Lands Beyond. Jess melted into that world, laboring for several years before going to school and becoming a teacher. But eventually the sorrow in his blood became like a thin, high singing and a sickness, and he could think only of purging himself in the waters of Atagahi.

"At times what is my doom becomes delight, for there's nothing like gliding in and out the clouds, letting the body twirl and swing on the currents. Yet it's still a curse, which robbed me of other, better joys. That it will now be lifted by death is a thought not unwelcome to me."

Birdie Ann shut her eyes.

Still as a mouse when the wing of an owl passes over its hiding place, Adanta held her breath. When she released it with a sigh, Tass leaned over and tugged at her sleeve.

"Your grandmother may be tired. Maybe we should go," he whispered.

"No," Birdie Ann said, her eyes still closed. "You must let my grandchild rest. I have salve for the leg. You and I, Tass, will collect the herbs for a sleeping potion. She needs a deep, dreamless nap. Sleep here. In the morning, after the dew lifts, we'll start out."

"To where, Grandmother?"

"The day before he died, Kalanu told me where the Lean One nests. He betrayed his kind and his vows to do so, but he did so willingly. However poor a father he made, he did that much for you and for Jess. I'll go with you, as long as my strength holds. I must. There's something more for me to do in this uncanny life of mine. If I cannot go, if I fall by the way, you must leave me."

"No. I could not do that, Grandmother."

"Yet you must. There are things we're sure that we

cannot do, but when the time comes, we have to do them. You'll need my help against the Raven Mocker. You'll need me to guide you. After we reach your mother, all of us must push on to find the Healing Lake. We have only seven days, and the first is but a fragment that passes away at dawn. That will leave six. Not long ago I saw your father—"

"Ba—"

"He's alive but very ill, much weaker than the last time I had seen him. It seems he begins to sense the lake, somewhere beyond him, still to the west. I had to find him. It was my duty to tell him about your grandfather. A father, no matter how strange, is to be mourned. I knew he would mourn, both for the man's life and for his death, but it had to be. He had to know."

"Have you seen Ba often since he left home?" Adanta was puzzled.

"He sent me, the day I came to you—the hour when you found me, or so you thought—in the corn maze. Kalanu had told Jess about the Lean One and your mother, and so Jess was afraid for you. At that time, his father would not say where the Lean One lived, though the man had attacked Jess and had stripped him of shirt and amulet. This broke the commandment to protect one's kind and freed

Kalanu to aid our son. You see? Bad as he was, he was still drawn to Jess and helped him against his own evil tribe. That they knew each other as boys, but the Lean One became a Mocker and my son did not: this is the reason that Astugataga hates him. Yet Jess is safer than when he was younger, because he is protected from the wrath of the Raven Mockers by his sickness; it is not a human illness but one of their own, a death longing that rises in the blood. It marks him as one of them, and it means that, in turn, he cannot harm or be harmed by them."

Birdie Ann gave the boy a swift, severe glance.

"It's good that you are here, Tass, because I don't know whether Adanta is secure among them, or even whether her naming of the Mocker will undo his power. My belief and hope is that the unraveling will be strong, more powerful than most, because she is, by birth, already one of them—but according to their traditions, she's still innocent, not yet come of age and prepared to claim her evil birthright."

"Mother said the Lean One was my godfather," Adanta remembered.

"Yes. It's as I said. In their world, it means a wicked promise—that he has vowed to rear you up to be a Raven Mocker."

The old woman hesitated.

"What?" Tass crouched down at her feet. "What are you thinking?"

"There's no doubt that he enjoyed pursuing Charlotte and toying with Adanta's dislike of him, but he may also have wished . . ."

"To lure Adanta onto his own grounds!"

"Yes."

"Then why did you let her come?" he asked, his voice rising.

"Because she must—"

"To save my mother," Adanta put in.

"Because she must stand against him and escape his clutch. Understand this, she may need—*will* need the healing waters herself. Only they can rinse away this sorrow in the blood."

"But the danger . . ." Tass stared across the room, to the window where the single pane now glowed a deeper amethyst.

"Yes. She must face it. The Lean One has pledged himself to make her one of them. He also knows that she could turn and destroy him before that change is complete, and so he will be on his guard and ready to fight back, should she rebel against him. But Adanta may have a degree of safety. The Raven Mockers will not allow their kindred in evil or their underage children to be harmed, not if they can help it, and they will avenge themselves, eye for eye, life for life, on one who kills his own kind. They are more than kin in many ways. Their wizardly communion, when they eat the hearts of the dead, is very powerful. It binds them as one, as do their gifts of invisibility, disguise, and flight. They are dangerous because they can pass unseen among men and women, though they hunt alone, seldom in packs. They all know about me, and they can scent the blood sickness in Jess, but I can't be sure that Adanta would be known by any but James. There were times in his childhood when Jess might have been killed had he not been Kalanu's son," the grandmother said and added, "I do not know for sure if protection descends to a granddaughter with an injured leg."

A HAUNTED FOREST

Half the day had flown before the three travelers dared the winds and rain outside the eyrie. The grandmother had been visibly weaker when she awoke, and it took her hours to gather strength. Adanta needed the rest as well. She lay on a bed while her grandmother showed the treasures of the eyrie—coverlets, the thread handspun and dyed, tightly woven. Lengths of cloth were stacked in her cupboards, and the wardrobes spilled over with handmade garments. She gave her granddaughter an apple-green dress with a rosy sash and a butternut-dyed undershift.

"It's all yours," she said, caressing the heaps of fabric.

Tass paced nervously, occasionally checking on Polk or striding along the porch and letting the gale knock against him. Rapids of air snapped his hair back, threw him against the railing as if it would hurl him down the precipice. When he thrust through the door, the screen swung madly against the cabin's outer wall. His eyes glittered, and his skin was wet and reddened, scoured by the gusts. The eyrie brought out the daring in Tass. He was eager to stay, to go—exploring, climbing the rocks, begging the grandmother to let him clamber out the dormer windows and up on the rooftop. Coming down, his face shining with spray, he said, "I have seen all of Adantis, I believe, and it is splendid—blue and cloudy—mostly cloudy today." The grandmother laughed and told him that he had seen only mist.

In the early afternoon, sun broke through, striking the suspended droplets and erecting an immense rainbow across the landscape. "One leg in Adantis; one in the Lands Beyond," Birdie Ann told them. Echoes of the bow—two, three more arcs—stood hazy and pale in the distance. While one remnant still hung like a banner above the mountains, Tass loaded the pony, folding three of Birdie Ann's blankets across the animal's back, fetching White Brow's cage, and adding a pair of lidded baskets joined by a leather strap. The contents of these plus what was added to Adanta's pack would have to keep them for the journey's length. The girl rode Polk, with Tass at his head to guide him with a word, a click of the tongue, a touch. Her grandmother walked, a sparkle-berry staff in one hand. She led them down the mountain by a trace so indistinct that it was hardly a path at all. The going was difficult, the leaf litter moist and slippery. Coming to a place where the trail forked, Birdie Ann took the left branch, and in a few minutes they edged along a cliff, then passed by some diggings that she said had once been an alum mine. Just below these, she stopped at a cairn of stones. Kneeling, she picked up a single shard of quartz and placed it on top of the mound. When Tass did likewise and then handed her up a pebble, Adanta set it down with a faint *clink*, wondering at her grandmother's labor, for in the tall pile were chunks like those in the shattered granite ledge nearby, but also others, feldspar and dolomite and lumps of sapphire that came from farther off. Layers of smoke-colored mica glinted between small boulders and had clearly been put there for ornament.

She did all this for him, though she never loved him. Kalanu. My grandfather, the raven. Robber of life, eater of the hearts of the dead. Adanta's hand trembled as she touched the heap of cobbles, chilly even in the sunshine. How could one even begin to say a prayer for a Raven Mocker? To forgive such a being—that was a mighty task.

Her grandmother kept on, did not look back . . . Adanta could not help but do so, watching as the cairn dwindled and was obscured by trees. After a while Birdie Ann paused, waiting for the others to reach her.

"Before I go forgetting, this unlocks the three doors of the eyrie. I won't be needing it anymore. Fasten it well." She slipped a silver key tied with a snip of crimson yarn out of her pocket, placing it on a shelf of rock. Adanta leaned from the horse to pick it up, thinking how strange and sad it was to have a grandmother one could not touch. Now, however, she understood the reasons why. And so the mountaintop place was to be hers! The house edging the long drop into the valley, the big rooms and stone fireplaces would be hers, and the cupboards of complicated weaving, worth a small fortune in the Lands Beyond. Her grandmother would never again sit at the loom in its sunny corner or watch the weather tumble willy-nilly from rain to rainbow to shine, never again see it brighten the window with one amethyst pane, for she would not be going home. It was hard to believe. Adanta smoothed the apple-green skirt. Her grandmother's hands had spun the thread, dyed it, warped it on the loom, thrown the flying shuttle, cut down the web of finished cloth—leaving a row of thrums still fastened to the loom—and made this gown. Maybe this was the only way she would ever touch her grandmother: at one remove.

By the time they settled for the night, building a fire and folding beds from the warm, horse-scented blankets, Birdie Ann was stumbling, her hands shaking. She ate nothing, letting Tass boil corn in the pot Adanta still carried in her pack. He spread the bedrolls on nests of boughs cut with Charlotte's knife. Kneeling close by the old woman's side, he whispered in her ear, and she returned a feeble answer.

"It's not my time. I will be better in the morning. We must go faster and farther tomorrow."

At dawn she was nowhere to be seen. After smearing salve on Adanta's knee and wrapping it in clean strips of linen, Tass slipped his hand inside the grandmother's caul of wool: it was no longer warm. She must have risen long before, her gown becoming feathers, her arms turning to wings. Eyes roving from camp to trees to sky, he prepared to leave, fastening Adanta's knapsack to the leather strap and helping her onto the horse. In her right hand the girl carried the sparkleberry staff. They did not speak of the grandmother's absence but moved quietly along the trail, the boy just in front, each knowing that they might never find the Lean One without Birdie Ann. The footing here was treacherous, and once Tass tramped unawares on loose stone, shooting downward about twelve feet, skinning and bruising his arm. Polk lurched and threatened to crash after him, then jumped, heels lightly grazing Tass's head. Caught in a slide of shale as he landed, the pony scrambled, feet scrabbling for purchase, while White Brow whistled a protest, her cage swinging from a knot in Adanta's sash.

When the boy half skated, half leaped to their side, Adanta lay plastered against the pony's neck, and Polk was taking in shuddering breaths.

"Let's do that again." She pushed herself up, giving Tass a small smile.

He stared at her, then laughed out loud.

"We don't do that, we Adantans. We don't say one thing and mean another. Unless we're bad. Or moon-mad," he added, "like Magpie Joe. Maybe you're a bit crazy."

Down, down they trudged. Once they glimpsed a glimmering figure and looked at each other silently. Hadn't the grandmother said that the western valley overlooked by the eyrie was more trafficked by Little People and spirits of all kinds than any other? The creeks and rivulets, charged by the recent storm, fired across the path, carrying a freight of mud and grit. Now and then they heard a thunderous explosion as one of these torrents vaulted from the mountainside, hurtling to the rocks below. The hills resounded with the songs of many streams. When at last they reached the valley floor, the two looked about, indecisive. Here the faint trail split, with no sign to guide them.

"When in doubt, eat." Tass unpacked some corn bread and dipped water from a brook with an ancient-looking glass bottle that he'd found in some weeds, rinsing it first. Through the wavery glass they watched the silt-laden liquid settle, sand and dirt drifting to the bottom. When she drank, Adanta thought it tasted chalky and strange. Although tired of riding, she didn't get down, not wanting to tax her leg with the effort of dismounting and mounting again.

"Now what?"

"Now wait, I guess. There's no time to shilly-shally. But not any for getting lost, either."

The blue-green mountains stretched for miles. Looking about, Adanta remembered how they had seemed to her when she lived in the Little Cottage In Between—like an endless swath, each ridge the same as any other. It was not so. Even here, where she had barely begun to learn the Adantan names, she recognized places her grandmother had shown her from the western windows of the eyrie. There was Kamama Gap, where the migrating monarch butterflies shot from the valley on upward currents. Sweeping her eye along the mountaintops, she saw the smooth rock face known as Kalanu Old Town, because ravens had once nested nearby, and close to it the pierced ramparts her grandmother had called Talatu Place, where the wind chirped through the rock like a thousand crickets. Someday she thought she would go there, someday when nothing but pleasure called her. And there were other butterfly chutes, abandoned raven townsites, and stones famous for their piping in the mountains, many known by the same names as these; she wanted to know them all.

"Should we just try one and hope for the best?" One of the trails headed due west, while the other rambled out of sight, its aim unclear.

"Ha!" Tass shaded his eyes.

Scanning the horizon, Adanta detected nothing.

"That spot. There—above the notch."

Nothing. She kept her eyes on the cut, straining to

see. Then, something—small as a gnat, it swam into view. It grew larger, a wavering point. Diving, it vanished against the background of leaves. The two waited, sharing another wedge of corn bread and dropping a trial crumb into the wren's cage. *There.* Riding the updrafts, a raven spiraled overhead, wings backlit by the sun. *Grandmother.* Adanta remembered Ba's stories of the Raven Mocker, shedding fire drops from its feathers. *And all the time, he knew himself to be a child—a chick, a nestling—of the Raven Mockers!* She wondered whether he had told her those stories to prepare her—or whether he simply loved the old tales more because of his own miserable link to them. Swooping, the raven circled Polk and swept forward, flying just above the crooked path until it became lost in trees.

Vaulting up behind Adanta, Tass slapped the pony on the rump. Their wait was over. On a branch hanging across the way perched the raven, watching them with shining eyes. *Tok! Tok!* They jogged on, the girl twisting to catch another look at the bird. The rut along which they passed was as crooked as a long unlatched chain dropped from a great height, twisting crazily and crossing itself again and again. "Wiggly and wingly," the boy remarked, using the Adantan term for such windings. Dizzying, the route took a distance "as the crow flies" and doubled, tripled its length. White Brow seemed to like the woods, hopping from bar to bar in her cage and trilling merrily. To Tass and Adanta, it was an uncanny place where the firs blocked out the light and the mountains— more like a journey underground. Strange hootings made them scrutinize at the forest canopy. Not far ahead, three perfectly naked children leaped onto the trail, jeering and pointing at the riders, then hopped into the underbrush. They were tiny, their limbs pale against the shadows, and fine hair floated around their heads. Without thinking, Adanta grasped her amulet. As they passed the spot, not a trace appeared of the three—as if they had melted into air. Thumping his heels against the pony's side, Tass urged him to hurry. The clopping hooves soon attracted the attention of another child, a young hunter with blowgun and arrows. He raced through the trees, parallel to the track, and managed to keep with them for a long time because their progress was so knotted. When Adanta suggested that they diverge from the track and meet up with it later, Tass refused, saying the idea was unsafe. The impish figure grinned at them, jumping logs and shouting "Yah! Yah!" but he never came any closer. At last, spying a playmate, he peeled off into the woods.

"Just a boy." Adanta leaned back to speak to Tass.

"No. Detsata. That was a part in Mooney I did not believe, but already I have seen enough to have trust in it all. I know now that what our own people forgot he wrote down and remembered for us. I just hope we don't meet some of his other spirit people or ogresses or giants."

Silvery laughter flooded the air, and again Tass urged the pony on. When they crossed a gap in the trees, he pointed to the sky, where the raven could be seen, sailing on the currents.

"She must have been too tired to walk."

"And she said we must go a long way."

"We've come pretty far already."

Dipping back under the leaves, they fell silent.

It was gloomy in this portion of the wood, although at the clearing the sky had been blue. Here it was as though a storm cloud had tangled in the boughs, so dark and low the ceiling above them appeared. The area was completely silent. White Brow trilled once and hushed, and the pony slowed, loath to continue, until Tass called to him and slapped his flanks. Murky and uneven, the pathway narrowed until they could touch the boles crowding on either hand.

"There's a light," Adanta whispered.

Sure enough, a wavering flame could be seen close to the trail, its gleam showing now and then in the narrow fissures between trees. It cast a glow on withered skin, a bony arm.

"Give me the staff." Tass's arm slid along hers until it reached the stick. At once striking the pony about the legs, he shouted "Hi! Yah! Hi! Hi!" Polk bolted down the corkscrewed path, the brightness rushing close behind—until with a yawn of fetid air it was snuffed out. Continuing to shout and beat the little horse as he veered wildly between trees, Tass let up only when they charged out of the shadows and into a sunlit meadow of scrub and rhododendron. Polk slowed, trembling and breathing hard, and Tass reached around Adanta to pat his head.

"I never hit my horse before."

"What *was* that?"

"I don't want to know. There's a spirit or a witch that people call the Fire-carrier. It traipses about in the dark, holding something that burns in its hands. Nobody who found out ever came back to tell what it is. The people just skedaddle for a sunny spot when they see that spark."

The raven, high overhead, drifted across the valley.

"That forest is spirit ground. I'm sure this is the

220

black area on the Adantan map where Ma told me never to go. It's a wonder I never came here before. Having her tell me not to do something is just like waving a red shirt at a bull. Of course," he added, "there are so many things she tells me not to do that it's hard to cover them all."

"Tass!" Adanta gestured upward.

Wobbling on the wind, the raven circled lower. She was no longer alone. A larger raven sped toward her, not riding the currents but beating his wings hard, his cries of *crrruk! crr-u-k! crr-u-k!* making a ghostly echo in the valley.

"Grandmother, watch out—"

"No—don't give us away!" Tass guided the pony to a hiding place inside a stand of rhododendrons.

The smaller raven crashed into an island of trees as the pursuer dived straight down with a shriek. Then there was nothing: silence. The two on the horse strained to hear, but there was only a soughing of branches from the haunted wood. Slowly they moved forward, creeping from one big rhododendron to another, still listening. Some minutes passed. They held still, fearing to go closer. At last a raven struggled from the treetops, lumbering into the air with a wounded wing, dipping and flapping low to the ground.

Which one?

Adanta kept her eyes on the green isle, but no other bird rose from that spot. Shrinking, the injured raven vanished in the distance. Tass lightly dug in with his heels, and the pony trotted on, bobbing his head, and White Brow began to chirp. The sun stepped out from behind a shield of cloud, sending a blaze of arrows across the valley. The grove behind them, they rode through a summer's day once again, but Adanta still felt cold and frightened. She remembered her mother slipping from the blue sill, and racing after her but finding nothing at all.

They were not far from where the ravens had dived. It had taken much longer to get there than they had anticipated. Abandoning the crooked path, Tass jumped down and was about to lead the pony through deep grass when Adanta stopped him with a cry.

"*Ku!* There, look there—not those saplings—under the lightning-struck poplar—do you see? There's something there."

The boy smiled—and kept on smiling at her until she leaned down and shook him by the shoulder.

"What is it with you? Go see. Go on. Please."

At this he sprang away, wading quickly through the tall grass.

"Miss Birdie!" His voice wafted to Adanta. She was sweet-talking Polk, trying to coax the pony to follow, when he returned.

"Let's sleep here. Your grandmother is hurting— she needs sleep. And we can't help her in any other way, since she won't let us touch her. She believes the Lean One will not have the strength to come back tonight."

"Then it was the Lean One! We must not have much farther to go. Why did he pursue her? She said that they would not harm their own."

"Not kill, maybe. But he attacked your father, too."

When Adanta saw her grandmother, she felt unsure whether the old woman could live another hour, she looked so colorless and frail. Her neck was bandaged, but blood seeped through the cloth. When she spoke, her voice was hoarse. She had flown a distance that morning, searching for and finding Jess, returning to seek out Adanta and Tass. It had been hard because she was weary and could no longer battle the whiplash of air; when the Lean One had come, bearing down on her with all his might, she fled and could only wriggle between close-growing branches, hiding while he sought her out. After his beak had pierced through her neck, she assaulted with what

force she held in reserve, hammering at his wing-
bones until he lurched away.

"Such as he seek out the helpless, and I am not yet
helpless," the grandmother whispered.

The birds' duel had not gone unnoticed, and some
curious Yunwi Tsunsdi gathered around, one of
them an herb woman. The healer, being one of their
spirit tribe, had not been afraid to pick up the raven
and rock it in her arms, treating the puncture with
sweet-smelling salve, bandaging it with cloth— "of
a curious weaving," the grandmother noted—and
placing it gently on a coil of grass. When the change
had come upon her, the Little People had scattered,
skipping to the haunted forest.

"And so you found me." The grandmother closed
her eyes and, like the wild creature she was in part,
sank instantly to sleep.

Tass tucked a blanket around Birdie Ann, careful
to respect her wishes and make no contact with her
skin. Then he helped Adanta from the horse and began picking up brush and boughs. It wasn't until
the camp was made—White Brow sleeping with her
head under one wing, Polk cropping the grass, the
blanket rolls prepared, Adanta's freshly salved leg
propped on a stone, and the pot on the blaze sending
up a fine stream of bubbles—that the girl remem-

bered to ask why he had smiled at her so when they
had stopped near the oval of trees.

"Oh, that!"

"Oh, that what? You beamed like a pure idiot. Like
somebody who has stayed lost way too long in the
Messers' corn maze."

"Don't you even know?" Tass leaned back from
the fire, and now he was smiling again. "You *don't*
know."

"No, I don't know." She snatched up a pinecone
and hurled it at him.

" '*Ku!*' You said it, don't you see? You're becoming
Adantan." He tossed the cone in the coals and sat up
to drop some ground corn and a handful of fresh-
picked greens into the pot.

"What on earth are you talking about?"

"You said '*Ku!*' You *said* it." He grinned, feeding
the flames a few more broken limbs. Afterward he lay
down near the fire, putting his arms behind his head.
"*Ku!* The stars are coming out—the winds must
have blown the clouds away."

Adanta cocked her head back and looked up at the
dome of heaven. *Ku! Becoming Adantan. It was something to think about . . .* There she was, sitting beside
a wounded Raven Mocker—her own grandmother—
and next to the Pony Boy, miles and mountains away

from her old life. But the stars, they were the same. The Pleiades and Betelgeuse, the North Star and Aldebaran, the Swan, the Twins, and Berenice's hair: her mother's voice, just beyond hearing, was telling over the bright names. Above her they raised a tent more bright and shining than the one in which Lalu, Teller of Wonders, had frightened her with a tale of a girl who swam in the healing lake and was changed forever.

To the Nest

In the morning the grandmother seemed entirely recovered from her wound, except for a scar that appeared to be weeks old. The powers of the Little People were great, and they regretted that Adanta, as well, had not been treated by the herb woman. The travelers struck camp at dawn and moved out, just in case the raven should return in search of Birdie Ann. The grandmother showed them the way to the Lean One's nest, carefully drawing the route with a stick in the dirt, pointing out each landmark. On the crude map a scratch climbed the mountain that lay directly before them, then followed the ridgeline. The grandmother's hand trembled as she gestured. She seemed weaker than the day before, but she was determined to go with them to the Raven Mocker's eyrie and then on to the healing lake. Although she walked for nearly a mile, she fell behind, waving at them to continue without her, wanting to be alone. Soon she was gliding on the air far above them, her wings ruffled by the wind. The path across the valley curled through scrub and only by slow degrees began to rise. When the sun centered itself in the sky, Tass and Adanta stopped to rest and eat slabs of cold, hard mush and dried apples. Afterward the girl took some tentative steps, leaning on her grandmother's sparkleberry staff. Jabs of pain flashed up her leg, but she kept on, and after a while the joint seemed to bend more freely and to hurt less.

"There is something more the matter than bruises and a bad cut that won't heal, maybe more than a sprain. I don't know. And it's my fault. I wish Red Betty could take another look at it." As he packed the baskets, Tass watched her move slowly along the trail.

"The leg doesn't matter. Just so long as I can find the Lean One."

It was afternoon before they gained the ridgetop, where a cold breeze carried the fresh scent of rain and earth and buffeted the raven still hovering above them. Pulling the stole from her pack, Adanta wrapped it around White Brow's cage. She and Tass rode on, blankets around their shoulders. It was sunny and clear over the valley they had just passed, but far to the west a mass of storm clouds rolled toward them. Polk trotted along more quickly now that he was at the crest; the path dipped and rose, and on each side they could see miles across the valleys. Off to the west blurry ink lines slanted down from thunderheads, and the horizon line was washed away by blue cloud and mountain, melted together.

The air quickened, batting the raven from spot to spot. Fighting its lunges, she swooped and landed on the sparkleberry staff, the ruff on her chest and her wing feathers wind-raked and wild. Clamping her feet on the crooked top of the stick, she gave Adanta one piercing, glittering glance, then thrust her head beneath a rumpled wing. The staff, fastened to the leather strap that secured baskets and pack, rocked back and forth, and the girl put out a hand to steady it. In this way the three continued on horseback, riding high, close to the clash of light and dark. By late afternoon the sky to the west resembled midnight, the deep navy clouds invading the valley. Once the raven peered from under her wing and cried out, as if against the coming gloom.

By the time they approached the Lean One's den, Tass had jumped to the ground and was leading Polk through a blue-black world. The raven flexed her claws, moved restlessly on the staff, and veered up into the gust as drops struck them like a handful of thrown pebbles. A downpour swept across the mountainside to the west, coming their way. Tass hurried on ahead, searching the dusk for the raven and for the Lean One's lair; he might have passed by had not the bird dipped and snared his hair in its claws just as he reached the place. Then he saw and sped back to Adanta, just as the curtain of rain blew onto the mountaintop. The girl shivered as she made out the door to the Lean One's lair, which resembled shelter for neither man nor bird but something in between. Thousands and thousands of slender boughs and withies must have been slashed and curved to make the swooping coils that joined several trunks, rising to the treetops. Holes pocked the surface of the nest, one large and close to the ground, most of the others high above—gaps that might be windows or inlets. A spindly light escaped from the openings, shining weakly against the neighboring firs.

Adanta remembered something the grandmother had said in the morning: not to stop and stare, should anything surprise them, not even to spare a moment for her own mother but to seek out and stride directly toward Astugataga and call him by his rightful title of Raven Mocker. The old woman felt more strongly than ever that because Adanta was not yet to the age of transformation, she would be able to break the enchantment—that the unreeling of the spell might be especially potent, coming from Kalanu's grandchild. She should not worry about injury, though he might attack before she could speak, seeing her vulnerable.

Despite the sodden blanket, she felt warm and glowing, perhaps from fear, from anticipation. She could feel herself becoming firm in determination, as if she were expanding slightly, taking on strength. Wings slamming the tumult of wind and rain, the raven homed to its perch. Adanta stared into a round eye glazed with water. She could do this; it must be done. Otherwise they might all be destroyed. Yet it was hard to do the thing, knowing that it meant death, even to one who was riddled with wrong. *What comes to him comes of his own evil*, the grandmother had cautioned. Yet without her saying the words, it would not come. The first death in that case would no doubt be her own. She thrust the fear of a change worse than death from her thoughts.

Tass helped her dismount, telling her to wait, wait until he tethered the horse—he was afraid Polk might scare in the storm or bolt down the mountainside if the Lean One showed himself. But she did not want to pause. As Adanta bore down with all her weight on the injured leg, the knee burned like a caged bonfire. With a gasp she pushed the pain away—set it aside. Now it was like a fire leaping on a hearth, close by but no longer scorching her body. Gripping the staff topped by the raven, she paused to look at the immense nest before crossing the threshold. The walking stick clumped on moss and stones, which gave way to worn planking. The roots and boles of trees were linked by more of the withies, woven in a swirling pattern; glancing upward, she saw that the high ceiling was thatched with reeds. A single light flared, by which she could see a flittering, batlike motion. She stumped on, the crude scepter knocking against the floor.

The hall widened, and at once the main chamber of the nest lay before her. There was her mother— *Mama!*—crooning to something in her arms, paying no attention as Adanta entered. The girl swept her eyes across the room. Crying and cawing, a flock of ugly creatures scattered, then, curious, edged back toward her. She paid them no mind, heedful of her grandmother's advice. With the crutch she thrust them out of her path, searching for the Lean One. From the darkness at the back of the cave, she heard a grating caw, and she pushed on, seeing him rise up on one elbow and give a laugh, half-jeering and half-triumphant, as he recognized who she was.

"You're mine, Kalanu's seed!" he crowed, raising himself up, his eyes winking like jet beads. "Mother of ravens to come—we'll snatch souls in our claws and slake our thirst with the cups of men's hearts and nest on the one branch forever and ever!"

He was naked, half-shielded by a bloodstained sheet. Crudely splinted and bandaged with rags, his wounded arm lay useless on the featherbed. Perhaps he saw something in her face that he did not like, or perhaps he was in anguish from the damaged limb, because for a moment he shuddered and set his jaw, gritting his teeth.

"Careful! You can't—" he called out, his voice soaring, and then the change was upon him.

Trembling, sweating—the pain from the leg sparking through all her limbs—Adanta drew close to the Lean One. Squirming on the bedclothes, he screamed as the quills pierced his arms. The wing-sheaths broke from his back, and glossy feathers covered his nakedness. Face still bare, size undiminished, he reared up on his knees and staggered to his feet, letting out a great war whoop as he raised a powerful wing, while the shattered one beat against the floor.

"You, the Lean One, James, Astugataga, curse of the innocent—I see you and say that you are a Raven Mocker, robber of life!" To her ears the voice was not her own; it sounded like an echoing thunder-clap, low-toned and powerful. The raven, her grand-mother, fluttered on the sparkleberry staff, crying out in the language of birds: *prrruk! pr–u–k! crrr–u–k!* Adanta stepped back. She glimpsed Charlotte's face, a pale flash in an archway, as with a single rearward glance her mother bolted into the shadows. Tass was shouting as he flung himself through the passageway from the ridgetop.

The air felt suddenly colder to the girl. Would nothing.happen? Would the Lean One be murderous in his anger? If there was no change, Tass would have to say the words once more. And if even then there was nothing, they might all die.

The dark, like a winged hoverer, seemed to be watching and waiting with held breath for what would or would not occur. Then at once breath was released in a rush.

Groaning, the Lean One dropped to his knees. Flame licked his wing-sheaths as more feathers ripped through his skin. He faltered, shrieked as the bones of his feet arched, becoming claws. Then, launching himself toward the roof of the nest, he scrambled onto the withies. Crawling slowly up their stems with his talons, wings flapping and shedding sparks, he collapsed on a platform, moaning and gulping air.

"You mortals can't harm me," he boasted, his breath rasping, his eyes fixed on Adanta. "I'm not like that one—a weak woman—one I found snooping about my nest—I pierced her neck. Kalanu's bride—the Hidden Mocker—grandmother to the foreign brat. Mother of Jess—*tok!*—friend of my childhood—who spat on—his own birthright—would not join us. No one else among the Mockers would care—about this woman—Charlotte—would care what happens to her—she will be my prey. As for the Hidden Mocker—may she die—soon. And you, girl, you'll be my mate—I'll rend you in my claws." His sudden laughter thrilled, like a plunge into a mountain stream. He leaned over the jagged lip, smiling at his accuser with still-human lips. "I'll tear you like a stolen heart—"

Before anyone could speak, he hurled himself from a breach in the wall with a scream, plummeting into the murk and rain.

Stock-still, dizzy and drenched with sweat, Adanta stared at the gap from which he had plunged. Now that her words were finished, she was panting, shaking as if she had slipped from a rock into icy depths and, lungs bursting, taken far too long to come up again. "Is he dead?"

Tass put a hand on the sparkleberry staff to steady it and craned his head, searching the exits to the nest. The grandmother had already winged upward and was sailing in and out the apertures of the nest.

"I never heard of a Raven Mocker being named when he was in the change. Something like that might kill him right off, for all I know. Or maybe it would do something else. Something worse for us. But I think we're safe, for now.

"*Ku!* What are these?" Tass yelped and kicked at the creatures.

"What? Where's Mama?"

For the first time the girl looked at the flocking birds. In an instant she took in what they were: large, fat-bodied beings with glossy plumage and the heads of children. Staring, she saw that they were like children's heads but not children's heads, for the faces looked old and dull of skin, more wrinkled than any human flesh could ever be, as if they had lived a thousand years.

Nauseated, she hung on to her support like an ancient to his cane, lowering her head. As she did so, they whirred into the air, croaking and flapping their wings. One brushed her face with its feathers.

"Horrible." Adanta pressed her forehead against the smooth sparkleberry wood. Her leg burned with pain, but she resisted it.

"These are—" Tass stopped, puzzled. "These must be his children."

"Not by my mother!"

"No, no, the children that ravens bore him, when he mated with the birds. His egg-children. What else could it be? These are some kin of Raven Mockers—look at their faces. He has fed them with unclean food—with the hearts and blood of his victims."

Here the children began to weep, the tears to trickle down the creases of their withered cheeks. Clustering about Tass's legs, they leaned forward as if to embrace him, but he pushed them off. They let their pinions down and sobbed inconsolably. One pressed its cheek against another's, one rested against a glossy neck. They drew closer, put their faces together. It was a strange and pitiful sight to Adanta, who shrank from them, tears in her eyes. The raven on the stick hid under its wing. Then it seemed their grief lessened. Singly or by twos and threes, the little kindred of the Raven Mockers bobbed up to nests in the eaves of the roof. There the cries slowly died away, one last child snuffling and hiccuping after the others were making only a faint peeping.

"Have I killed them? I named them—will they die?"

"I suppose so, Tass. It's terrible to say, but they never should have been born, should they?"

The boy stared at the ceiling, where the creatures were settling for the night, turning and cooing.

"No, but I never meant to hurt them. What did they do to us?"

"It's done. What else can we say? And who would feed them, without their father? Maybe it's best. Or maybe we're wrong. Maybe they'll fly to the Haunted Forest and live with the ghosts and fairies. The spirit people might care for them. They belong there, more than any other spot."

Limping away, Adanta poked her head through one opening after another, but could not find Charlotte. She and Tass called, but no one answered. The raven flew to the wall of withies, her head cocking as she searched the nest. Only when she had needled through all the passageways did they find Charlotte, cowering in a corner, a bunched blanket in her arms.

"Mother, it's me, Adanta."

Charlotte's eyes were glazed over, blank as a window with nothing behind it.

"Please, Mama—do you hear me?"

The woman clutched the bundle to her breast, backing against the withies.

"What do you have? Can I see? Will you show me?"

This time she glanced nervously at the girl but still did not seem to recognize her. Turning away, she carefully adjusted the cloth. Adanta braced herself, prepared to see one of the Lean One's children—to see some wrinkled, cooing infant in her mother's arms. Or perhaps there was nothing but fabric. Or something horrid, something that would make them tremble and gape for breath. Swinging around, Charlotte pulled the covering back. An infant beamed up at them, dimple-cheeked, its glossy eyes roaming from face to face. It is hard not to smile at a happy baby, and so Tass and Adanta smiled.

"Sometimes, when a woman takes a wizard or spirit husband, a child is born right away, not like it is with the rest of us." Tass gave Adanta a sideways glance, uncertain how she might take such an idea.

"No, look! It's not like that. You were right—it *is* half bird. Look under her hand. It's like the others, only not old. See? Shiny black feathers."

"I saved this one." Charlotte whispered, her voice rapid. "*He* brought me here, and he saw I liked them. He poisoned the others, spoiled their beauty. He didn't want me to pay attention to them, and he marred them so that they scared me. But he was still more frightening than they, except sometimes when he looked handsome and young. One by one, he took them away from me. He made them like himself, so I couldn't look at them. It made them cry when it happened, when they saw that I could not bear to see them and kiss and stroke their faces as I had done before. I still rocked one in my arms sometimes, but I had a horror of them. I couldn't hide it. Only this one I always held and never let go. I didn't love him better than the others until they were ruined, you see. I loved them all. This one was the smallest. After the others were changed into something else, I wouldn't let him sleep in the nursery because then the raven would come and feed him poison. I couldn't stand for them all, every one, to be wrecked. They were all I had."

"You had me, Mama." Adanta's fingers brushed her mother's hand. The sorrow of her mother's loss of the bird children seemed deep as a well—into which the girl could feel herself falling, the distance between them increasing at every second.

Charlotte didn't seem to hear but kept staring at the woven roof.

"Astugataga—he's gone. I don't think he will come back." Adanta said the words twice.

"Gone," the woman repeated, "he's gone."

"Yes."

When the raven gyred downward on quiet wings, Charlotte screamed—a short, stabbing cry. Adanta watched as her grandmother sailed back up to the ceiling and vanished into the gloom.

"Just a bird," she told her mother. She blotted the tears from her cheeks with the sleeve of her dress.

"What do you call your baby?" Tass bent down, his eyes on Charlotte's.

"Little Bumblebee. That's what I call him. Do you think it's a good choice? I couldn't remember any children's names."

"It suits him. It's a boy, then?"

"I'm not sure. I thought it had to be because . . ." She appeared confused.

"Because you already have a girl, perhaps?" Tass suggested. "Here, this is your daughter. Her name is Adanta."

"No," she whispered, twisting the ring on her finger, "I never liked that name."

"Maybe your husband chose it."

Charlotte stared at him. "Really?" She sounded doubtful.

"*Ku!* I never lie about important things. I wouldn't fib to you."

"Some people do." Slowly she raised her eyes to his face.

"Astugataga lied, didn't he? But I don't. I have a good mother, one like you. I tell the truth." Tass tickled the baby's chin and made him wiggle inside the swaddling. "I'm going to get my pony out of the rain. When I come back, I'll build a fire, and I'll dry our blankets and cook a hot meal for all of us. No poison. We'll sleep here tonight because it's raining hard. In the morning we'll leave this place. You and me and your daughter, Adanta, and her grandmother—she is close by—and your baby, Bumblebee. Then you can go back to your real home, or you can go wherever you like. Is that all right?"

Hesitantly, she gave a nod.

"Good. That's settled, then."

Adanta followed when he got up, lurching after him.

"She has some sort of Raven madness," the boy told her.

"She likes you better than me." Adanta touched him on the arm, as if she were pleading with him.

"Not really—it's just the bird sickness that makes her forget who and what she is. We'll have to find someone who knows such diseases. Maybe I'll ask the Messer witchmaster, now that we're cousins." Tass put a hand on the staff, his eyes on the mother and child across the room. "Go sit with her, or she might take it into her head to run away."

Charlotte sat smiling down at the baby.

"Do you remember me now, Mother?"

Giving her a sidelong look, Charlotte said, "No."

"But I came to find you and Ba."

"You found me." Charlotte laughed, making the baby coo and thrash his wings. "Bumblebee wants to fly, but I've been afraid that the bird would steal him."

My mother doesn't remember Ba. The thought was a fresh pang.

What should she do? Adanta had never thought past discovering her mother. If she found her, everything would be fine—that was how it had seemed to her when she had set out from home. She'd never dreamed of such a sadness as this. To have a mother who could not recall waiting for her child to be born or standing in the grass while her daughter took a first step, could not even remember all the evenings sitting about the kitchen table—Ba reading aloud to them while Mama whittled. To have a mother who had turned her heart away from her own and to a strange little creature like a feathered cherub! But she needed her Bumblebee, that was clear. She must have clung to his warmth through the terrible hours with the Lean One. Perhaps if they went back to the Little Cottage In Between, her mother would remember their old life together. The baby could bobble about the rooms and chase real bumblebees in the garden out front. Her mother would see the pictures of herself with Adanta, growing up, and with Jess. Her hands would be drawn to the bears and rabbits and fish she had carved in earlier days.

The knife! When Tass came in with the dripping baskets, cage, and pack, she dug deep in her pack.

"Look and see if you can find some wood worth whittling in the pile by the fireplace," Adanta called, and in a few minutes he came up with a smooth-grained piece and laid it next to Charlotte.

"Do you recognize this?" She held the handle of the knife toward her mother.

She said "No" but picked it up anyway. It seemed that her hands remembered, because she began carving. Peelings heaped at her feet. At first Adanta was afraid that she would whittle and whittle until hills of shavings mounted up—that she would carve until there was nothing but air under her fingers. Soon it was evident that she was making something. It grew under her hands. There was a wing, then another, and it became a baby-headed raven. A raven-bodied infant. Laying down the blade, she dangled the toy over the child.

"He's so good. I had to keep him very quiet. He let me, once he saw what happened to the noisy ones."

The wings fanned in excitement. The bird feet snagged and then kicked off the light blanket. The baby fluttered into the air and zoomed around the chamber, dipping and somersaulting while Charlotte shrilled, pleading with him to come down, come down before the raven man came. Chortling, he dropped into her arms, and she squeezed him tight, rocking back and forth, eyes shut.

Closing the knife, Adanta reflected sadly that outside of Adantis, this child would be a sideshow freak. Inside, he was certainly curious but not something to be bought and sold, as he might be in the Lands Beyond; Charlotte might lose him out there. Anyone who stumbled upon their cottage would be astonished, perhaps frightened. Who could blame them? He was born of great evil. But it seemed that there was nothing wrong in him. If there had been something wicked in his infant being, her mother's love had driven it away.

It occurred to the girl that she had a choice now. They could go home, yes, and perhaps that would prove best, but there was another possibility. There was the silver key in her pack. She imagined them moving from the Little Cottage In Between, Polk pulling a cart loaded with their household goods over the mountain, she and Tass and anyone who would help—possibly the giants—carrying a load. With Adantan gold she could hire some Messer horses to drag their belongings over the ridges, up the winding trails. She could bring everything that had once meant home to her mother: the carved marriage bed, the chairs and table, the albums and pictures, the lamps and—no, not all the lamps, just the kerosene ones and the store of candles. Nothing that called for electricity, because the grandmother's eyrie had none. They could live in that mountaintop house. They wouldn't have many visitors. Bumblebee could play on the porches, and if he rolled off the edge of the precipice—what of it? His wings would carry him safely. No one would kidnap him there, shut him up in a circus or a laboratory. Slowly the peacefulness and the fresh air would restore her mother. Then, someday, Charlotte might want to leave Adantis and return to a world where there were no feathered babies, no Raven Mockers, no outlandish cries rising from a haunted wood. Or perhaps not. It would be her choice, when her mind was right. Birdie Ann would help, with her wisdom, her suffering that was older and longer than Charlotte's. She envisioned the two women becoming friends, her mother whittling a bird or bear while her grandmother cast the flying shuttle, building a world of color on her loom.

No, not that. Adanta remembered that the curse of the Raven Mockers still lay heavy on her grandmother. That recollection, the breaking into her dream of the eyrie made her gasp out loud. As the feathered baby's eyes flew to her face, the vision floated entirely away. Today was the third day after the one when Tass had called out in warning that the old woman was a Raven Mocker. That made four days. There were three days left, three days more that she could spend with her grandmother—and somewhere out in the rain and the pitch-dark of night wandered Ba.

THE LAKE

When Adanta awoke, the ridgetop was an island moored in a sea of cloud. Even the haunted grove was obscured from sight, and Adantis seemed truly a world of Hidden People. The grandmother, returned to her human form, was cooking breakfast on the fire. Rocking, Charlotte sang an odd tuneless song to the baby in her arms. And moving about restlessly, head cocked back, Tass tried to see if the other children were still in their beds. *Pruk! Crr-uk! Prr-u-k!* he croaked, but no answer came. During the night, mist had seeped through the gaps in the nest and settled near the roof. Under the eaves the air was hushed, as skies on a fair windless day are hushed, when there are no birds in sight.

"I'm afraid they're dead." He squatted on the

floor, eating the bowl of mush the grandmother had placed at his feet.

"Perhaps they were wakened by the damp air coming in," Birdie Ann suggested. "If they heard us talking and understood, they might've flown off to search for the forest. They belong with the spirit folk, after all. Who would want to stay in this polluted hole? Later on, if I feel strong enough for the change, I'll fly and see. If not, you'll just have to live with not knowing." She stirred the pot, humming Charlotte's song.

"This room feels cursed. I can't help picturing them, the years passing and nothing but feathers and bones up there." Tass put down the half-eaten mush. "Or maybe you're right. Maybe we'll meet them again in the haunted woods."

Adanta watched, noticing how slowly her grandmother moved this morning. She was even weaker today, closer to the seventh day, the day marked for her death. It had also become clear that the change from bird to woman and back was leaching the life from her. After breakfast, when the clouds were untangled from the trees and laurel thickets in the valleys and began to float skyward, the grandmother and Tass and Adanta discussed what was to be done. It hardly seemed that they could take Charlotte

along when their hopes of finding a healing lake
might be only a chimera.

"But perhaps it will make her well," Tass argued.

"Not according to the old stories, the ones passed
down. They say that the lake heals blood sickness
and wounds and injuries; it may cure some other diseases. But never do they promise a healing of the
mind or a cure for such Raven madness. It might
even be dangerous for her—those who have peculiar
thoughts and longings can be transformed into new
shapes." The grandmother turned her hands upward. "Who'd risk such a change? I say *no*. She
needs rest, she needs the counsel of witchmasters.
Take her home to your mother, and let Adanta and
me proceed alone."

"What if—" Tass broke off in mid-question.

"We can't worry about the Lean One. I believe he
must be dying even now. And we can't fret about the
poor child's leg. We must go on, no matter what. It is
not far to the cove where I last saw Jess. He's traveling without hurry, searching carefully. He believes
that he is very close to the lake. And he doesn't have
many days of life left, unless he discovers a cure. We
can make it to wherever he is. I won't be returning,
but Adanta may come back with her father, should
he find the lake. Who can say whether he will? Not

we mortals. Only the Spirit that gives us courage can tell."

"That's what the witchmaster talked about—the Spirit." The girl's eyes shifted to her mother and the baby jiggling in her arms. "I think you are right about Mother. She likes Tass now. And I wouldn't want Ba to see that she has forgotten him. And me."

Nodding, the old woman went on. "Tass, take the horse, because you must gallop through the enchanted woods with its ghosts and spirit-creatures. If not, you may be harmed by the Fire-carrier or by some witch or wizard. Then our striving to save Charlotte will have been in vain."

"Miss Birdie, what about the walking, what about Adanta's knee?"

"I can do it. I'm sure." The girl spoke firmly, reaching for a walking stick. "And I'm taking White Brow with me to the lake."

"The leg doesn't matter. There's no time to spare. Even if it grows worse, what can we do but treat the wound and hope? Listen, this is what you must do. Take Charlotte over the mountains to your cabin. Rest and tonic the pony, and give him praise for his bravery. Prepare food to last ten days. Come back with your father; he must ride a powerful horse, one strong enough to bear two grown men through the forest. That is in case Jess returns. He's thin and starved, not much burden, and you and Adanta can ride Polk. But before that, you and your father can camp at some agreed-upon landmark on this side of the Haunted Forest—"

"I know," Adanta said, seizing on the grand-mother's words, "the whistling rock. Talatu Place. I'd like to go there. It's so high up, you can see it from the ground or from the ridgetop and probably from the next valley."

"At Talatu Place," the grandmother agreed. "Then you wait, Tass. And you stay until they arrive, or un-til she does, alone. If no one comes—we won't think of that. She'll return. You'll fetch the two or the one. That's all."

"Yes, I see that it's a good idea. Maybe the only way." Tass glanced up at the cuplike nests coiled from withies. "I don't like this raven's lair, but I don't want to go—I feel as if I'm abandoning you both."

It was an hour before they were prepared to leave, the food divided between the two parties and a fresh staff cut for the grandmother. She was too weary to make the change this morning. When it was time to part, Tass held Adanta's hand, then hugged her hard.

"I've been hasty about the wrong things," he confessed, "but no more. I'll be back."

As he could not touch the grandmother, he simply held her gaze for a moment and bowed deeply before leading the pony away, Charlotte riding with the child snuggled against her neck, the pair of them swaddled in a blue blanket. Mother and child did not look back, but the boy did, many times, calling for them to take care.

"That one, he's a courtier of the hills," the grandmother said, "a real Adantan."

When the figures were lost in trees, the two started down the other side of the mountain, Adanta with her pack and White Brow's cage, Birdie Ann with blanket rolls. Everything they carried was needful, carefully considered. The one thing that seemed a luxury was the book, pen, and ink, but somehow Adanta could not bring herself to send them back with Tass. Climbing downhill, bracing against the pull of gravity, was rugged work for the injured leg, so the two moved haltingly and rested often. Besides, Birdie Ann was unfit for hard walking. Even White Brow was sluggish in her cage, clinging to a perch without moving for hours at a time. The girl asked her grandmother about many things she had not been able to ask before—about Birdie Ann's childhood in Adantis and the family she had not seen in years, about Jess the baby and boy and young man, about the weaving that was her life's labor and pleasure. It might have seemed like an ordinary day had they been seated on a porch, rocking and chatting.

Not far down the mountain, as they navigated a narrow trail on the lip of a precipice, the old woman wavered, leaning out over the chasm so that her granddaughter shouted a warning.

"Look!" the grandmother called. "There!"

Creeping to the edge, Adanta peered below. Dizzy at first, she could hardly make sense of the scene before her. Then she understood. Farther down the drop, a gigantic raven with twisted wing had smashed on a promontory of rock. Straining to see, she made out a human wrist in a cuff of feathers and a half-transformed face.

"The Lean One," she whispered. "Astugataga. And this is my doing. I killed him, Grandmother."

"All our books tell us the same: those who sow evil reap evil. The blame is not yours." The grandmother's eyes closed, and she began chanting, her hands out: "*Ku!* O Spirit, someone has stepped over the soul of the Raven, the Lean One, Astugataga. Forgive that one in her innocence. His breath, his spittle is at rest on the stone. Someone has covered him over with a black cloth. Forgive that one in her ignorance. Someone has covered him with black slabs, never to be seen again. Accept that one in her penitence. Toward the black coffin in the darkening land, Astugataga's paths stretch out. The black clay covers him. He is lodged in the black houses of the darkening land. His soul has faded. It is becoming blue. In dusk his spirit dwindles. O Spirit, he is your child. Remember him. Look down upon him where he lies, the color of twilight. In the moment his soul was shadowed, did he cry out to you? Remember with mercy that man, a sinner. He is altogether blue. Someone has stepped over his soul. Restore that one to purity, that she may see the waters of Atagahi. Remember this one also—Birdie Ann, Mother, Grandmother—that uncleanness and taint be cleansed, O Spirit."

The invocation washed over Adanta, reminding her of the strange legacy of intermarriage between the half-wild borderers and the Cherokee, their sacred beliefs blending together. For many hours she thought about the meaning of the words, and about how the Raven, the Lean One, had called down the color blue on her mother in the woods near the Little Cottage In Between.

In the afternoon Adanta walked alone, bearing both pack and blankets after the grandmother had slipped away to the rocks, absent for a long time before the change was complete and she circled overhead. Coasting above the treetops, she sailed off in search of her son. Within three hours Birdie Ann was back, lighting on the sparkleberry staff.

The girl could go no farther. Her knee was swollen again, streaked with red. The raven hopped along the ground, showing Adanta the smoothest path to a stream, where she soaked her leg and washed the bandages. Without eating, she made a bedroll and tumbled into sleep, long before night. The bird had insisted that she start a fire, bringing dried grasses, twigs, and small branches and arranging them in a tepee—poking at her blanket until the girl fetched the wooden matches from her pack. The last thing she remembered was the raven, dragging a thin bough to the flames.

At dawn she woke in considerable pain, and it was midmorning before she could put weight on the leg. She limped less than half a mile before unpacking the bedroll and crawling inside the blanket. She felt sick and shivery and could not eat, although she drank some water from a nearby stream. When the grandmother flew away and returned more quickly than ever, she knew they must be very close to Ba, but the least pressure on the knee made her moan and grit her teeth. The bird walked around and around the camp, restless, bringing twigs to a fresh blaze. After a while she collected many soft dried grasses and wove them into a curious tight whorl, more a basket than a nest, with a pattern like a sunburst at the base. Even as raven, Birdie Ann was still a weaver. Adanta wondered whether her grandmother could no longer transform into a woman. It was sad to lose a day's companionship. The sixth day. Perhaps it was best spent as a bird. She pictured a gliding on the currents, a sudden thrashing of wings, a light toss upward from an invisible hand. If only she could ride the air like Birdie Ann! She would not be able to keep climbing and searching much longer. She would have to return as she had come, keeping her eyes on Talatu Place. If she could not walk, she would have to crawl. Rather grimly, she told herself that she would make it, even if she had to drag herself forward by her fingernails. The thought of the grandmother's approaching death and her own loneliness overshadowed all else. Too tired to speak, she turned on her side, putting her thumb through the vines of White Brow's cage. Hopping down, the wren pecked at it lightly. The little bird had not trilled all morning.

If, as Tass had said, growing up was measured not by numbers but by daring the world—doing deeds, braving regions that one had never known—then she must be getting quite old. She stretched out a hand toward the woven nest, her gaze meeting the raven's lustrous eye. She noticed that when the bird nestled down, the feathers around her throat made a ruff, shaggy and thick. The two stared at each other beside the flames until Adanta, all of a sudden drawing into her bedroll, fell asleep.

When she woke in the afternoon, she remembered that tomorrow was the seventh day. Oddly, she felt nothing of the dread which had held her still and stiff a few hours before. Pulling away the blanket, she saw that the leg appeared worse, angry and inflamed. She looked around, leaning on an elbow. The nest was empty. Grandmother, in human form again and busy cooking at the fire, called out a greeting. While her granddaughter had slept, the old woman had prepared a poultice of bruised Solomon's seal roots, which now lay mounded on leaves. After hobbling to the stream, Adanta washed the bandages and applied the paste, binding it with wet strips of cloth. The grandmother worked quickly, rolling balls of mush cooked with shreds of dried meat, wrapping them in leaves but offering her nothing to eat. Afterward she tucked them into her freshly woven basket like so many green, frilled eggs.

"For tomorrow," she told Adanta.

The girl's purpose was fixed. She knew that without her grandmother, she might never find Ba, might become lost trying to discover him. She must press forward—it was not far, although the swollen leg made even a few steps seem much too long. It did not matter. She would have to set the pain aside. Again it would be like a bonfire sparking and shooting stars, but not so close that she could think of nothing else. She must keep her mind distant from its heat and flickering torment—it was the road to Ba she must consider, step by step. They would not have to climb, for they were near, very near, and lakes, after all, flowed in the valley, not on mountaintops. She could, she must do it.

When the campfire was scattered and the last glowing embers sprinkled with dirt, they set off, following the stream's path. As she hobbled, Adanta from time to time could barely make out a humming sound, which the grandmother said must be the beating wings of wild ducks, drawn to the healing lake. When she craned her head to see, shielding her eyes against the glare of the sun, she could distinguish nothing. Staves in hand, the two pushed forward, the grandmother tottering in her weakness, the granddaughter limping, dragging her injured leg. They journeyed for almost four hours, until they came to a dry flat where there were no songbirds, no animals, not even a single blade of grass—only a few heaps of boulders. The stream that they had followed petered out here, sinking into the earth. Adanta stopped, listening, her eyes on the stone cliffs above the valley. Faintly she could hear the whirr of wings.

"I think we should camp here for the night, Grandmother."

Birdie Ann gazed at the lifeless expanse of packed soil. Without a word she folded the blankets into seats and gathered wood, walking along the stream to an island of tall trees. Bent low under a shock of sticks and branches, she made her way back to the girl and built a fire in the grass near the flat.

"Are you hungry?"

Adanta shook her head. The heat in her leg seemed to have mounted to her face, and she felt flushed and sick to her stomach.

"For now, that's fine, but tomorrow you'll need to eat—there will be time enough then. Tonight you must stay awake. Somewhere close by, Jess will be awake as well. I can almost feel him, he is so near. He has not eaten in many days. And now we have not eaten. We must keep vigil in the old way, as the first settlers did for the dying and newly dead and as the Cherokee did to sharpen their eyes. To see such sights as the enchanted lake, one must fast and pray. The Spirit comes only to those who prepare a dwelling place."

Dusk poured out of the forest as the coal of sun slipped downward and was extinguished in the darkness behind the mountains. When wind blew the clouds away, it left a sky burning with stars. Blankets over their shoulders, the girl and her grandmother sat silently through the night. Released from the cage, White Brow hopped about in the firelight, hunting for spiders. Adanta tried to set her mind on the words she had learned in the village church, long ago, but soon it strayed. Orion and his bears seemed to twinkle in sympathy as she remembered the pilgrimage from the Little Cottage In Between—she could see Mama slipping from the blue windowsill, the Messers' corn maze, and the queerly hatted figure of Magpie Joe bobbing along in the scrub— could see Tass lounging outside Mrs. Terrell's tent, talking to the children of the song-bows—could see

the giants and Lalu with fireflies in her hair—Caledonia, with her robust goodbyes—the spirits of the
Haunted Forest flashing across their path as Polk
galloped toward the meadow beyond—the Raven
Mocker's nestlings, clamoring underfoot, and the
Mocker himself, angry, the wing-sheaths erupting
from his shoulderblades. It all felt close and touch-
able, and yet entirely strange. She half believed herself on that journey still and not camping here,
near what surely was her goal. The struggle through
Adantis now seemed to her more splendid, more terrible than she had realized before, and she remembered the book and ink in her pack, resolving to
write it all, should she live and make it back through
the haunted woods. One after another, those she
loved and those who had helped or had threatened
her on the way visited Adanta as she sat, her head
tilted, her gaze on the skies. *Ku! She had been on the
Spirit's path all along, it seemed.* A tear wet her cheek,
but she did not wipe it away. The faces came as thick
and fast as falling leaves on a yellow day, until she entirely forgot herself, staring up at their starry eyes,
their shining hair.

It might have been hours she sat like this, or it
might have been only minutes. The sun wove its rosy
colors through a warp of dark-blue trees. Some-

where freshets were trickling, spouting, spattering. Her eyes dazzled, Adanta glanced away from the fading stars, toward the flat. Like an ocean shorebird, the grandmother was skimming across the ground, bent low, her shawl flying behind her. As she fled, drops were dashed up from her heels.

Grasping the staff, the girl swayed to her feet.

A wide shallow lake brimmed on what had been the dried mud flat, its sheet of purple glimmering in the distant shadows and reflecting the light of dawn. From the cliffs on either side sprang jets of water, thundering into the valley. Instant by tidal instant, the expanse deepened in hue as it rose.

Atagahi.

Like many small rainbows, the arcs of fish flipped in and out of the current. The noise of cataracts mingled with a great whirring of flocks. Ducks and pigeons swooped and turned, settling on the surface. A bear lumbered from the depths, shaking his pelt and slinging spray in all directions.

Ba!

She could see Ba now, the grandmother hauling him up out of the waves, his head flopped to one side.

"Grandmother!" the girl called. She limped into the flood. A turtle bobbled against her calf as she moved deeper, and something foamed and sparked on her sore feet. When she reached knee-level, she moaned in surprise: a white-hot anguish shot out in a sunburst of spears, radiating from the injury.

"Ba—Ba—Grandmother," she shouted.

Laying her son down, arms out, on a jut of rock, the old woman looked up.

"It's too late—he was already dying—he's almost gone."

Adanta's knee gave way beneath her, and she plunged into the lake, dropping the stick, which floated away.

"Ba, Ba—"

She surfaced, spitting out fragrant mouthfuls, and sank again. Rising, balancing on one leg, she sang out in astonishment, "Look, look, Grandmother; look there." Among the trees danced a tiny figure with glistening stars in her hair. *Lalu?* Whoever it was, she was stamping her feet and pointing to a nearby rock face. Adanta scanned the banks opposite. Out of a gap under the cliffs streamed a company of men and women, tall and straight and shining. The grandmother stepped back as they came forward. When they called to Ba, he sat up—when one took his hand, he staggered to his feet. A waist-deep white fire coursed around him. Now they were gesturing to the opening, and slowly he was wading out of reach, a bright wake shimmering behind his body.

"No," Adanta wailed, "Ba, Ba, I can't bear it—don't go."

He turned like a man in a dream, his eyes lighting on hers, and he stretched out an arm. The Nunnehi began filing through the stone door, until only a few remained.

"Let him go," the grandmother pleaded, stumbling toward Adanta. "He is too close to death—what is one dying touch when he has held you in his arms so many times? Let him go. Few are chosen by the Immortals. The way will shut fast in a moment."

The girl paused, longing only for her journey to end in her father's embrace. Had she come so far only to give him up?

A chickadee ricocheted over the wave crests, trilling *tsikilili, tsikilili.*

"Come." The last of the Nunnehi spoke from the door.

"Yes," Adanta cried, "Ba, go, go to him." The sick man looked across Atagahi at his daughter but did not speak. When he turned away, she reached out her arms toward him, remembering the evenings when she and Mama had listened to him read aloud or tell stories. Ba waded far from her—farther—and was helped up the slope to the door. In a moment, he, the party of Nunnehi, and the entrance all vanished, and there was nothing but mountains and outpouring flow.

"I didn't even get to say that I loved him," she whispered.

Weeping, half-angry at Ba who had left her and at the grandmother who had urged his leave-taking, the girl caught hold of the floating staff and pushed herself off the lake floor. Abruptly she stopped crying and stood up.

"The pain—the pain's gone." Drawing up her waterlogged skirts, she stared at the injured place. It was no longer red or swollen. The slash across the knee had puckered and healed, leaving behind the shape of a crescent moon, barely visible.

As she stared, she heard a splash and realized that the grandmother had tripped and had plunged underwater. In another moment Birdie was up, choking and paddling feebly toward a ledge; there she held on, floating. Throwing the stick aside, Adanta waded out to her.

"You're well." The old woman leaned against the shelf of stone. "That's good. Listen to me, my dear and only grandchild. My time—it's here."

The girl drew back.

"No, Grandmother. This is the enchanted lake. You are healed, aren't you?"

The grandmother rested her gaze on Adanta's face.

"Some things," she said slowly, "cannot be cured this way. Just as your mother could not be. I have been washed by the medicine lake. I have seen the Nunnehi come forth from their townhouse in the rock. That's enough. It is my hour. This morning has drained me of strength. I cannot resist. I am ebbing."

How could she die? Adanta's eyes were glazed with tears, and there was an ache in her chest that no healing magic could burn away. The grief was for Birdie Ann and Ba and for Charlotte, so altered that she was no longer *Mama*, not really—and for herself, she who must return alone, mourning the lost and the dead.

The grandmother let go and drifted on the face of the pool.

"Take me in your arms," she said. "I can't hurt you now."

Adanta cradled the old woman, marveling at how small she proved to be, how delicate and frail. And she the same one who had rushed across the lake, heaving Ba out of the drowning waters!

"I loved you," Birdie Ann whispered. "All your life I watched from the trees—every hour I could steal from Kalanu—from the day you were born in the downstairs bedroom of your first house. I was there in the dead oak tree when Jess carried you out in the yard to see the sun, to be held high enough to see the mountains of Adantis. The shadow of my wing crossed your glance that morning. You reached your fist up, as if you wanted to steal a feather from the bird's tail."

Adanta was telling the grandmother that she, too, was loved, when the whorl of water around them started to shine. The old woman slipped out of her grasp as easily as a fish, and when a panicked Adanta thrust her arms under the surface, she found nothing. *Nothing.* She stared down into transparency. A stream of bubbles rose, and like a dart aimed from underground, the raven-her-grandmother shot straight into the air. Shedding drops, she circled the girl's head once and soared before weakening and gyring downward; then suddenly she plummeted like a stone headfirst into the deepest part of the lake.

The waves roiled uneasily for a moment; then there was calm again.

As echoes of Adanta's scream broke up above the valley, the noise of thundering lessened. The water-spouts and fountains slowed on the cliffs—slow, slower, stopped. All trickling died away. Steadily Atagahi receded. Dawn light gave way to morning sun. Birds arrowed into the sky, veering over the cliffs. The level was sinking, was to her waist. White Brow, flicking violet tears from her wings, swooped to Adanta's outstretched hand and perched. The girl saw that the tiny bird could now go free, the injured wing healed. What use was a cage now? Even White Brow would leave her. As the lapping dwindled past her hips, she hurled the creature into the air with all her might, calling out, "White Brow, fly, fly away home." The pond—for so it now was—drained farther. To her knees. To her ankles. The fish and turtles and ducks had disappeared. The mud flat began to dry. In a moment, there was only a single purple puddle on its face. As Adanta hurried toward it, the liquid shrank, and there was but a patch of dampness that she, kneeling, covered with one hand.

A whiteness flitted behind the trees, laughing with a sound like bells. *One of the Little People? Lalu?* Only a spirit could revel so, after what had happened in Atagahi. Shyly, the figure came forward, stopped, skipped onto the mud flat, and darted to the spot where the raven had vanished into the lake. Grasping up something slender and white in each hand, she danced back to the cliff. There she capered for joy, a short, whirling pirouette. Easily mounting the steep slope, she jumped a log and vanished among the trees. An eerie, ethereal music drifted into the valley.

Curious, Adanta crossed the flat. There, where the raven had dived, lay a white flute—a small bone flute pierced with holes. She picked it up and placed the mouth to her lips. Enchanting, the notes made her shiver.

The "all-overs"—that's what Adantans would say.

She turned the flute in her hands. Was this, then, all that was left of her grandmother's body? It was lovely in shape and glinted, faintly sparkling.

A sign of healing, wasn't it? As when waves first washed against the knee. White. The color of joy.

Remembering a piece of advice Tass had once given her and not knowing whether she had the right to have the flute—for surely the wild fairies would desire such a thing and might be angry if she took it—she called out, as he had told her to do. "Little People, I want this. May I take it?"

A quiver of laughter rent the air.

"Bone of my bone," Adanta cried, suddenly re-membering Lalu's words, "bone of my bone—the debt is paid!"

She began walking toward the last night's camp. Seized by the vigor of health, she started to bound and race, the flute in one hand. A curl of breeze lifted her damp hair, and the sun warmed her back. She knew what she would do. After she packed, she would go to the cliff and press her ear against the stone, for in Mooney it was said that one could thus hear the Nunnehi murmuring. Perhaps she could make out her father's voice, feel the warmth of his hand against the stone. Then she would set off dancing—jumping—spinning and skipping like the Little People. She might run all the way to Talatu Place, and there she would meet Tass's father for the first time. She hoped he would bring a fiddle or mandolin. Tass had said that he always traveled with at least one instrument in a knapsack. And she would be sure, Adanta promised herself, to tell Tass how much he meant to her—she would never wait too late to tell anyone, ever again. What she would then do, she did not know, except that she would never give up Adantis, nor the eyrie. There would be many choices to be made, many hours of coaxing Charlotte to soundness of mind. She would have to decide what to do about the Little Cottage In Between. For now she thought no further than the ridge-top landmark of pierced rock. It would be good to stretch her muscles, to flee across the valley and climb the mountain, to scamper up to the clouds. If Tass and his father had not yet arrived, she would camp alone next to high heaven, writing in her grandmother's book and playing the flute—letting it sing out heartstruck sorrow, joy, loss, and all the bold strength of her youth—the ravishing notes spiraling over the valleys and mingling with the sounds from the piping stones of Talatu Place.

AN ADANTAN GLOSSARY

An Adantan's language is a stew made from Scots, Irish, English, and Cherokee influences. Few Adantans remain fluent in Cherokee, the language having merged with the colorful talk of the backcountry settlers. Where it persists, the Adantan form of Cherokee most closely resembles the Kituwah (kee-TOO-wah) dialect of the Eastern Band of Cherokee. (The two have remained isolated within the mountains and have changed less than the Western, or Oklahoma, Cherokee dialect.) The hybrid English of Adantis—a nineteenth-century creation of settlers and Cherokee—binds the Old to the New World.

ADANTA (ah-DAHN-tah) Soul.

ADANTIS Adantis is called the "soul place." It lies deep in the mountains of western North Carolina and eastern Tennessee. It can exist only where the earth is not chopped and scraped for gain; it is the secret home of the Adantans, the Hidden People.

AGILI (ah-KEE-hlih) Agili is a name meaning "He-is-rising." Mooney says that it might be a short version of the Cherokee name Agin-agili, or "Rising fawn." It is also the name of a historical figure,

"Major George Lowrey, cousin of Sequoya, and assistant chief of the Cherokee Nation about 1840" (Mooney).

AGAWELA (ah-kah-WAY-lah) "Old Woman." In the sacred formulas of the Cherokee, she is corn or the spirit of corn.

ASTUGATAGA (ah-STOO-kah-TAH-kah) This Cherokee name means "standing in the doorway" and contains the suggestion that the man himself is a kind of door. Astugataga is also a hero in Adantis and in Cherokee history. On September 15, 1862, during a Civil War battle at Baptist Gap, Tennessee, a Lieutenant Astugataga of the Thomas Legion was killed in a charge.

ATAGAHI (ah-tah-KA-hih) The "Gall Place" or mythic lake of healing. "The name is also applied to that part of the Great Smoky range centering about Thunderhead mountain and Miry Ridge, near the boundary between Swain county, North Carolina, and Blount county, Tennessee" (Mooney).

BORDERER Adantans regard themselves as borderers. Many of their ancestors came from counties in the north of Ireland and those along the Scottish-English border—the Scottish lowlands and the northern English counties.

CORN WOMAN The corn spirit. Cherokee myths tell of Kanati, the Lucky Hunter, and Selu (SAY-LOO), his wife. They lived in the mountains long ago, when the world was new. Her name meant "corn." In death, she gave life to the world: where her blood moistened the ground, the first corn shot up. She is also called Agawela.

CULLOWHEE A mountain town on the Tuckasegee River. The name is Cherokee for "valley of lilies." The university in Cullowhee is home to Horace Kephart's notebooks, photographs, and writings. The Mountain Heritage Center often presents accounts and handicrafts relating to the Adantans, although these are entirely unrecognized as such by the curators.

DETSATA (DAY-tsah-tah) This runaway sprite of the woods hunts with a blowgun and sometimes teases human hunters.

ELAHIYI (ay-lah-HEE-yih) or ALAHIYI (ah-lah-HEE-yih) The name remains cloudy and mysterious. "This word could not be explained by any of the shamans to whom it was submitted" and may be linked to words meaning "south" and "earth" (Mooney).

FIRE-CARRIER, or ATSIL-DIHYEGI (ah-TSEEL-dee-HYAY-kih) A sprite or witch. She is thought to be dangerous and is sometimes seen carrying a light.

FRANKLIN A small mountain town in Macon County named for Jesse Franklin, once a governor of North Carolina, 1830–31. Originally the place was an ancient Cherokee settlement on the Little Tennessee River. Downtown Franklin is the home of the Nikwasi Mound.

FROG-GIGGING The catching of frogs with a small sharp spear or with hooks and a hand-line.

GALL PLACE Atagahi, the lake of healing.

JUDACULLA ROCK A pictographic rock. The Judaculla (or Jutaculla) Rock is located in a field not far from Cullowhee, North Carolina. The name is a corruption of Tsulkalu (TSOOL-kaa-luh).

KALANU AHYELISKI (KAH-laa-nuh ah-yay-LEES-kih) The Raven Mocker. He or she is a wizard or witch who robs the sick or dying of life, taking on a fiery winged shape and hunting for prey. After a killing, the Raven Mocker steals the victim's heart and eats it, thus adding the dead person's unlived years to his own.

KAMAMA (kah-MAH-mah) Butterfly.

KEPHART Horace Kephart, author of *Our Southern Highlanders* and instrumental in the creation of the Great Smoky Mountains National Park. He was a friend to Adantans, and some of the more cryptic references and names in his journals refer to Adantans and their ways.

KU! (kuh!)   An exclamation such as "So!" or "Now!"

LALU (LAH-luh)   The jarfly, or *Cicada auletes*. Lalu's midsummer song announces that beans are ripe, with green corn soon to follow.

LAUREL HELL   An almost impenetrable mass or tangle of rhododendron (especially the big rosebay rhododendron), lovely in bloom.

MOONEY, JAMES (1861–1921)   Passionate ethnologist and author of the books *Myths of the Cherokee* and *The Sacred Formulas of the Cherokees*, reprinted with a biographical introduction by George Ellison in the Lands Beyond (Asheville, N.C.: Historical Images/Bright Mountain Books).

MULLYGRUBS   Emotional upsets.

NIKWASI (nih-kwah-SIH)   Sometimes defined as "the center." Its meaning was declared lost by James Mooney.

NIKWASI MOUND   A large mound in Franklin, North Carolina. Here the Nunnehi had a large, invisible townhouse.

NUNNEHI (nuhn-NYEH-hih)   The Immortals who assist and protect the Cherokee in times of danger. Although usually invisible, they may choose to show themselves to those they consider friends. The singular form of the word is *Nayehi* (nah-YEH-hih).

POLK   An Irish family of high rank. The Polks held great power in the American "backcountry," intermarrying with leading families in North Carolina, Tennessee, and elsewhere. Its most notable member was U.S. President James Knox Polk, but Presidents Zachary Taylor and Andrew Jackson were also linked by marriage to the Polk clan.

RAVEN MOCKER   See Kalanu Ahyeliski.

SASA (SAH-SAH)   Goose.

SNAKE HANDLER   A low-church Protestant who believes that the New Testament asks the believer to "take up" real "serpents." The snake handler is a type of believer uncommon but occasionally found in the mountains inside and outside Adantis.

SONG-BOW   A simple musical instrument of bent wooden bow and string or wire. The string is plucked or picked, with the mouth used as a resonance chamber. The song-bow is simple enough to be made and played by small children.

TALATU (taa-LAH-tuh)   Cricket.

TEWA (TAY-WAH)   Flying squirrel.

THOMAS LEGION   A Confederate legion in the Civil War. According to Mooney, the Thomas Legion was composed of "two regiments of infantry, a battalion of cavalry, a company of engineers, and a field battery." It included four companies of Cherokee warriors who served primarily as scouts and home guard in the mountain borderland of North Carolina and Tennesse. The entire legion was composed of about 2,800 men, led by Colonel W. H. Thomas.

TSUNIL KALU (tsoo-NEEL-kah-luh)   A tribe of giants from the west who long ago came to visit the Cherokee. Tsulkalu was a slant-eyed giant who farmed Tanasee Bald.

UKTENA (oo-KTAY-nah)   A horned serpent, with diadem.

UTSIDSATA (oo-TSEE-dsah-tah)   "Corn tassel" or "thistle head"; probably "the Cherokee name of the chief known during the Revolutionary period as 'Old Tassel' " (Mooney).

WILUSDI (weel-oo-SDEE)   "Little Will," a fatherless child adopted by Yanugunski. According to Mooney, his birth father "was related to President Zachary Taylor" and "came of a Welsh family which had immigrated to Virginia at an early period, while on his mother's side he was descended from a Maryland family of Revolutionary stock." Little Will became a frontier trader, an agent for the Eastern Cherokee, a North Carolina state senator, a turnpike and railroad founder, an organizer of the Thomas Legion, and the chief of the Eastern Band of Cherokee until 1867. For more than fifty years, Wilusdi or Colonel W. H. Thomas was what Mooney calls the "most trusted friend and adviser" of the Eastern Cherokee.

YANUGUNSKI or YONAGUSKA (yah-nuh-KUHN-skih) "The most prominent chief in the history of the East Cherokee . . . a peace chief and counselor . . . prophet and reformer." Mooney tells an interesting story about the chief and his white neighbors. "On one occasion, after the first Bible translation into the Cherokee language and alphabet, some one brought a copy of [the Book of] Matthew from New Echota, but Yonaguska would not allow it to be read to his people until it had first been read to himself. After listening to one or two chapters the old chief dryly remarked: 'Well, it seems to be a good book—strange that the white people are not better, after having had it so long.'" Mooney describes Yanugunski as Cherokee with "a slight strain of white blood on his father's side," who adopted the orphan Wilusdi, or Colonel W. H. Thomas. When he died, he left behind two wives, children, and Cudjo, a "negro slave . . . devotedly attached to him."

YUNWI TSUNSDI (yuhn-wih tsoon-SDEE) The Little People. These are the fairies of the Cherokee.